THE
SONG
OF
JESSE

RICHARD J. NICHOLS

(Author of *Epic Stars of Long Ago*)

Fulton Books
Meadville, PA

Published by Fulton Books 2024

ISBN 979-8-88982-709-2 (paperback)
ISBN 979-8-88982-710-8 (digital)

Printed in the United States of America

To Frank L. Turley, a great man and an even greater friend. Thanks for the years spent together.

Prologue

THE CELEBRATED EPIC, *The Song of Roland*, is one of the oldest known poems in existence. Written in the eleventh century, it is believed to be authored by Turold—or Turoldus—and is a *chanson de geste*, old French for "song of heroic deeds." Of the supposed author, mentioned by name at the end of the poem, nothing is known. Experts are divided on the belief that the man is actually the writer of the epic, covering several pages of finely worded script and written in early French.

The poem relates the saga which happened on August 15, 778, in which the rear guard of King Charlemagne's army was attacked by a horde of Basques—inhabitants of the Pyranees—Muslims—who were opposed to the threat of Christianity as it was being forcefully spread across Europe by the vast throngs of Charlemagne's great mobilized forces, as in accept and believe or be killed.

Led by Charlemagne himself, a man who at one time achieved sainthood and who was of great esteem, even as the pope, the army devastated a great portion of Europe by virtue of sheer numbers and armament. The Battle of Roncevaux Pass involving the great French knight, Roland, took place in Spain. Roland, the leader of Charlemagne's rear guard, is thought to be a highly fictional character, but that thesis remains uncertain. Fated to be killed in the epic, he became a symbol for all Christians who were willing to die for beliefs fostered by Jesus Christ in the meridian of time.

The saga began when the Muslims inhabiting Saragossa in Spain, the last stronghold of the Basques at that time in that country, realized that they couldn't stand against Charlemagne's behemoth of an army and sent word to the great king and leader that they would relent before his opposing force and agree to become Christians. They also offered him the treasures of the city as his own if he would in turn refrain from destroying the city. The proposal met with some disdain from the Frankish leaders as some who were familiar with the people of Saragossa and their history of warfare feared that the proposal was a ploy, a trick to put the army of Charlemagne in a vulnerable situation where defeat was possible.

During the discussion by the council of leaders, Roland suggested that his stepfather, Ganelon, a man with whom he had been at odds in the past for various unknown reasons, should take word to the Basques that their offer had been accepted. The council approved the suggestion, and Ganelon, highly agitated by his role in the drama and fearing that the Muslims would kill him, reluctantly agreed to take word of acceptance of the agreement to the opposition. He did so, and they apparently treated him with respect and dignity as a courier and diplomat.

Before he left the Muslims, however, Ganelon, in a sharp reversal of character, explained to the Basques how they could ambush the rear guard of Charlemagne's army, led by Roland, at Roncevaux Pass in a daring assault and deal great harm to the powerful armada that was sweeping across Europe. They listened and agreed to the ambush. Thus, Ganelon, spurred by a desire to spite Roland for naming him as the messenger to take word to the army at Saragossa of acceptance of their proposal, placed not only Roland but also Charlemagne's entire rear guard in danger of imminent death.

As a result, Roland—portrayed in the epic poem as a wonderfully gifted French knight, the epitome of chivalry himself, full of pride and unfailing conviction in the cause of Christendom—was set up to be exposed to an inferior force of nonbelievers, considered pagans by Christians everywhere. Imagine the greatest knights of that time leading up to the Renaissance, and Roland would most certainly be among the greatest of whom history is replete.

He wore the famous sword, *Durendal*—meaning hard, a hard scimitar or scythe—given to him by Charlemagne himself, a gift reputedly given to the king from angels. It was the sharpest and strongest sword in existence at the time and could destroy hundreds, even thousands, without being vanquished. Legend has it that the famous sword was made by Wayland, the gifted Norse blacksmith who also fashioned other swords of incredible power. His horse, *Vielantiu* (old French, meaning vigilant), was a large, powerful steed, wonderfully muscled. Perhaps his armor was also fashioned by that same legendary blacksmith, Wayland, adding mystique to the aura of the valiant knight.

In the end, however, the Basques, by dint of overwhelming numbers, gained the upper hand in the conflict with Roland's rear guard. Imperiled by the suddenness of the ambush, his troops scattered, and without help from the main part of Charlemagne's army, the great leader Roland began to blow his oliphant—an elephant's horn—to call for help from the others. That action prevailed nothing as the main part of the army was too far away to be able to help. In the end, Roland died, blowing his oliphant until his temples burst from the effort. Before he died, the valiant knight threw his mighty sword against the nearby wall of the Pyranees so that the enemy couldn't have the magical weapon. The powerful instrument stuck in a crack and remained imbedded, a symbol for all who admire courage, zeal, and the conviction to be involved in a cause worth dying to achieve, in Roland's case, a martyr for the cause of Christ. The sword has since been retrieved and can be seen today in the Royal Armoury of Madrid, Spain.

For his treasonous act, Ganelon was later tried and found guilty and suffered an ignominious death. As part of his perfidy, thirty of Ganelon's kinsmen were also executed in the belief that those who bore his name could also bear his shame in consequence of the three thousand or so soldiers besides Roland that lost their lives in the ambush.

The story that follows could also be called a song, a saga of significance to those who believe in Christendom or a similar cause that is just. The characters are allegorical figures and represent others who lived ages ago. It is fictional, just as the life of the great French knight is believed to be fictional. The reader will have to determine for himself or herself what is fact and what is fiction.

Introduction

A GREAT DEAL has been written about the life of Christ, his miraculous birth as the Son of God, and of his ministry, later comprising roughly three years, from ages thirty to thirty-three. From recorded scripture as well as the annals of history, we've learned of Mary, Christ's mother, how she was highly favored by God, a choice virgin, young but willing to submit to God's will. We also learn of Joseph of the house of David and of his willingness to do as an angel had instructed him and take Mary as his wife since her pregnancy was not of man but of God.

Following his birth, little has been revealed about Christ the youth and of his formative years prior to his ministry. We are given to know through the study of the scriptures…*"that the child grew, and waxed strong in spirit, filled with wisdom: and the grace of God was upon him"* (Luke 2:40 KJV). We also learn from study that as he visited the temple at Jerusalem with his earthly family, the boy Jesus was missed so that in backtracking to the temple, he was finally located, still at the temple, speaking with learned men of his day, doctors…*both hearing them and answering their questions.* In the account recorded by Luke again, it reads, *"And Jesus increased in wisdom and stature and in favor with God and man"* (Luke 2:52 KJV). It is significant to note that Mary and Joseph had searched for the youth for three days before they finally found him. His reply to them at that time was instructive: *"And he said unto them, How is it that ye have sought me? wist ye not that I must be about my Father's business?"* (Luke 2:49 KJV).

As indicated in the recorded verse, born to Mary and Joseph were other children. Sons are mentioned, specifically James, Joses, and Jude. There were sisters as well but not mentioned by name (see Matthew 13:56 and Mark 6:3 KJV). His brothers are mentioned in scripture as advocates for Christ and his godly nature and calling, particularly James, who was a high church official in Jerusalem and was the author of the *epistle of James*. Jude also authored a short epistle, recognized by his name, preceding the *book of Revelation* in the *New Testament*.

The novel which follows relates to the childhood of Jesus as the firstborn son of Mary and as the eldest of the family of Mary and Joseph and is wholly fictional in nature. It presents the author's imaginative attempts at constructing what could have happened with Christ the youth before he became the Messiah, the Anointed One. In doing so, I have linked the boy Christ with siblings, both brothers and sisters, along with his mother Mary and his foster father Joseph, the carpenter. It depicts life with Joseph as a carpenter's aide. It dramatizes his life with Mary his mother as he progresses in wisdom and stature with God, preparing himself to become recognized as the Son of God by those who classified themselves as believers or followers of Christ later.

In the novel, the young lady represented as Mary Alice Houston becomes a symbol or personification of the biblical character Mary of Magdala, whom Christ blessed during his ministry: "*And certain women, which had been healed of evil spirits and infirmities, Mary called Magdalene, out of whom went seven devils*" (Luke 8:2 KJV). After the exorcism or healing, she became a devoted follower of Christ, was with him during his ministry, was at his feet while he was on the cross, and was also at the tomb when he was resurrected. According to the scriptural account, Mary Magdalene was first to discover the empty tomb, and according to John the Apostle—*he that Jesus loved*—she was the first to see the risen Lord (John 20: 11–18 KJV). There was a special relationship between Jesus and Mary Magdalene as reflected in those words of John.

Christ, according to his lineage as a descendant of David, was rightfully the King of Israel. One of the names given to Christ was *the Stem of Jesse*, Jesse being the father of David, former king of Israel. I chose to refer to Christ in the novel as Jesse because of that relationship. I referred to Mary, his mother, as Anne Maria. Anne in Hebrew means *full of grace, favor*.

Mary, also in the Hebrew, means *beloved*. Both Anne and Mary—or Maria—are descriptive of the mother of Jesus. I refer to the personification of Mary Magdalene as Mary Alice. Alice is a common name meaning *noble* and *of light*. Mary Magdalene was certainly noble in supporting Christ throughout his ministry. In that manner, she was also full of light, having received such from the Master. For Joseph, Mary's supportive husband, the foster father of Jesus the youth, I have chosen the name Isaac, meaning *one who laughs or rejoices*, since he had reason to rejoice following the visit of the angel, scripturally recorded in Matthew (Matthew 1:19–25 KJV).

The reader must remember that the work is purely fictional, portraying Christ as a young man of character and good works at an early age, prior to his actual ministry. It is also an effort to portray Mary Magdalene as a person of noble character with qualities similar to those of the biblical individual, Mary of Magdala, that became so important later in Christ's ministry once she was set free of the demons that had throttled her before meeting up with the Savior.

Miracles that occur in the novel are relative of such that took place during the ministry of Jesus. The reader can look for parallels between what is written here and what took place in Christ's life, particularly the raising of Lazarus, Christ's beloved friend, and brother of Mary and Martha, whose family was so endearing to him during the three years of his ministry. The miracle performed for Isaac in the novel has no parallel, however.

I have no special appointment or license to write about the Son of God as a young man as I perceive what might have happened, nor do I have a degree or degrees in theology. I do have an abiding interest in the man, however, and hope that abiding interest finds its way into your heart as well.

Contents

Chapter 1

An Intruder in the Home?

JAMES WAS A particularly talented young man. He enjoyed a keen mind, he was quick-witted, and had a love for others, along with a thirst for knowledge. At fourteen years of age, he had a good deal to learn but was satisfied that he had time to absorb all that life had to offer, everything truly important in life. The important thing was that he harbored a vivid desire to learn and treated each occurrence in life as a learning experience.

He had many of the facial features of his mother, who was wonderfully graced by beauty, a beacon in an opaque world. He also had some of the features of his father, the prominence of nose, ears, and lips that had come to define his character as the man had become an accomplished builder of homes, working outside, a slave to hard work and the vagaries of nature. James would eventually become a little taller than the other as he was then nearly six feet in height, well toned, and showing the promise of a strong, muscular body.

His tanned face was topped with a mat of dark hair. His rather perpetual scowl signified the wonder with which he assessed each circumstance that made its way into his youthful life, obstacles, challenges, family and friends, and what significance he should assess to each. He had a dark mole high on his cheekbone on the right side of his face. Other than that, he had no blemishes to his skin. His eyes were light brown, matching his skin coloring.

He had two younger brothers and sisters with which to grapple with as the family had advanced in years, making him the next to oldest. There was an older brother—a half brother really, an individual of sixteen years, whose birth had never been wholly explained to him. He did know that the boy was the son of his mother but not of his father, and yet that was never talked about, except to say that the event was without offense to either party, whatever that meant. How that was possible without some kind of extramarital affair being in the mix was a concern to James and to others old enough to delve into the primogeniture of things but one they were told not to consider and that the time would come when it would be explained more in depth, when they were adult enough to understand the explanation. He did know that the youth—his name was Jesse, meaning *God's gift* (and that connotation had created some questions, also that could not be answered quickly)—was highly favored of his mother particularly, so much so that the others sometimes felt left out, at least in part, when they were considering their individual worth in contrast to what was usually shown to *Big Brother*, as he was sometimes called by the others.

It was Big Brother who was always asked to help their father when he was involved with framing and finishing homes, along with other building chores requiring strong arms and hands, together with a sturdy torso with which to support a considerable amount of weight, or strain, as the situation demanded. James felt strongly that he was old enough and mature enough to be able to take the place of Big Brother whenever the other couldn't be quickly fathomed because he was sometimes given to doing things that carried him away from others, like he was in school, in some undisclosed place, learning from some unknown or even unseen person. In times like that, he wasn't always available to help when needed. Still, his father didn't call on James for help. It was as if he spurned his help, rationalizing that if he couldn't have Jesse, he would simply do it himself without help from others.

That was bothersome to James, even though he had learned to live with the notion of his inferiority to his half brother, so far anyway. In that process, he was still attempting to cope with the concept that was often radiated that the older boy could commit no wrong, that he was without any personal faults, that he was perfect, as nearly perfect as a mortal can be anyway, which they all knew was utterly untenable, but it was there anyway. He was presented to them as that rare individual who was never wrong, that always made the right decision, could never be second-guessed. That such a thing was impossible, didn't seem to be a consideration, at least to his mother. Still, that was the notion that surrounded Big Brother, that he was infinitely superior to others in whatever circumstance or situation that occurred. It was ridiculously unfair to James and to the other children, but it was a constant, nonetheless, and the others were taxed with the burden of having to live with the boy and show him love and consideration, which he apparently didn't need.

Looking deeper still, whenever Jesse was near their mother, he was always given the benefit of the doubt as the favored son, the one who was, without question, the gift to the family; the person that was never demeaned, punished, or even scolded for wrongdoing. Just the opposite, he was held up as the example of the insanely precocious child, the one all the others should follow without exception, no matter what. It was nauseating at times really; no one could begin to be as good or as resourceful as Jesse.

And yet no one had any knowledge of his schooling, who it was that was his mentor, his teacher. He just simply disappeared now and then, and when he came back, he was smarter, more resolute in matters of morality and the law, more astute overall. Whereas the other children, James included, could only resign themselves to being taught at home by their parents whenever they could find the time to rigidly follow a schedule of learning. It was a crudely devised system of learning, which didn't suit all of them anyway since they were so far apart in age but which was demanded of them at present because of conditions in which they found themselves, living in an area that was largely undeveloped, commercially and economically speaking, without established teachers or schools.

James and the others were continually aware of the double standard they were being held to in contrast to Big Brother as the family grew in numbers and, ultimately, reached their full complement. As they had grown older, James and the younger children had formed a strong bond within themselves which didn't necessarily include Jesse since he was older and given to a good deal of solitude whenever he found the liberty to do his will. James, for one, had developed a strong relationship with John, two years younger than himself, and with Jeralyn—usually referred to as Jeri—who had just turned thirteen. Together, the three of them had begun to help by assuming a small portion of the development of the two younger ones, Joseph and Jana, ages eleven and nine. That bond had grown more pronounced as Big Brother had spent more and more time helping his father and away in solitude. It also gave them more time to question their relationship with Big Brother.

It was at that time that James began to foster a resentment of Big Brother, speculating about his birth and stature in the family, as a threat to his own, almost. He took it upon himself to try and find out more about his curious birth, how it was that he came to be a recognized member of the family. He emboldened himself to question his father, Isaac, attempting to open his mind and delve into the secrets that were hidden so deeply but without success for his father had offered no clues as to the birth of Big Brother at all. Despite the setback, he continued to seek for answers. He was driven to learn all there was to learn about his enigmatical brother. He had questions that had to be answered, he considered: Just who was Jesse? Where was he born, and who was his real father? How did he manage to end up in this family, and what was the substance of the relationship between his mother and Jesse? Why did the youth spend so much time in solitude with no one else to converse with? Why was he here, and how long did he propose to stay? These and other questions occupied his mind so intensely that, at times, he felt like a stranger himself, wondering if he were the misplaced one, the one who had gotten lost at birth and who didn't belong. It was a riddle without an answer.

Worse, the youth began to think of ways that he could expose Big Brother. After all, there was no such thing as a perfect person, especially not now when life was so very difficult with plagues and sickness abounding, with political unrest and turmoil, with wars and threats of wars occurring daily, with hate and unrest swamping the nations of the world, with serious questions surrounding climatology from the North to the South Poles. There had to be an answer, and he meant to find it. Was Jesse a part of the problem, or was he the answer, as crazy as that seemed? He intended to find out.

Chapter 2

The Problem of Becoming Totally Honest

ISAAC AND ANNE Maria were together at home. The younger children had retired for the night, and James was with his friend, Bailey, and was staying over with the other boy with their permission and would be home the next morning. The two boys were studying together, or so they said, although neither parent truly believed that studying was the basis for their request but that it was a pretext for something slightly more covert, like how to have some fun in a ridiculous manner at someone else's expense.

Anne attempted to put into words her thoughts about the situation: "I'm not sure that those two boys are being totally honest with us."

Isaac had the same feeling but wasn't sure he wanted to explore the thought. "He seems like a good kid, doesn't he?"

"He's polite all right, and his parents are new to this area but apparently well regarded. I have the sense, though, that he's putting on an act of some sort."

It was nearly bedtime for the two adults. Isaac had lingered in the living room longer than normal without preparing for bed so that he could talk with his wife and not have their conversation overheard. He wanted to steer the conversation into another avenue but felt an urgency about the relationship between James and the other boy too.

"What do you mean?" he responded after a brief interlude of silence.

"I'm not sure. It's a feeling I get that he isn't quite the same on the inside as he is on the outside. Do you understand what I'm trying to say?"

Anne Maria was nine years younger than her husband, who, at thirty-nine, was a veteran of military duty and of community service, including a term as vice-regent or deputy at the sheriff's office, and more used to evaluating the merits of others with whom he had associated.

"I get the same feeling," he replied haltingly, "but I don't think he's bad, just that he's trying to figure out where he fits in with others, what is expected of him, and how to respond."

"I hope you're right. I look into his eyes, and I see something else. I'm not sure what it is…like maybe 'I'm putting something over on you, and you don't even have a clue what it's about.'"

"Oh, I wouldn't worry about Bailey as a friend. At least I hope James is able to take care of himself despite the situation. He knows better, I'm sure of that."

"Let's watch him closely, okay? I don't want our boy to get steered in directions he shouldn't to the point that it affects the rest of his life."

"I think you're overreacting, Anne, but yes, we need to watch him closely. We certainly don't want that to happen."

"Thank you, Isaac."

"Speaking about being totally honest, I've got a suggestion to make."

"You do?"

"Yes." He had been thinking about how to approach the subject, but since she had brought up the term *honesty*, that seemed to be the opening he was pursuing. "The children—especially James—have been talking rather extensively about the relationship between themselves and Jesse. More and more, they are wondering just how that relationship developed and what exactly was your part in the relationship? Do you dare talk about that with the family now that we've got children who are old enough to understand how that affects them? I know they're being placed in rather embarrassing situations with their friends who are asking questions that can't be answered."

She was silent for the space of several seconds, her hands cradling her face. "Who is it that's asking questions?"

"Well, James mostly, but I know they're all wondering now, especially since the older ones are being bombarded with questions."

"Isaac," she pleaded, "you know as much about the situation as I do."

"Yes, but the answer needs to come from you, Anne."

"Why does it have to come from me?"

"Because you're the only one who can explain how you had a child when there was no father…"

"But there was a father…"

"Yes, and that needs to be explained to their satisfaction."

She looked away and then back, attempting to hide her lack of understanding as noted by her distraught face, and tried to speak: "What if I don't know the answer, Isaac?"

He struggled with his reply, sure that a logical answer could be found but not knowing how to elicit that response: "Then, Anne, let's talk about the situation until we can come to a reasonable solution and find an answer that will satisfy the curiosity of the children and be acceptable to the hosts of others who are wondering the same thing."

Her frustration clearly showed. "I don't think it's possible, Isaac."

He was trying hard to maintain control, remembering all that had occurred when he had agreed reluctantly to marry her, knowing that she was pregnant with someone else's child, being a mere child herself but following through on a betrothal established through parentage, an odd custom in their two families that had carried over despite its obsolescence in current societal circles.

"Let's talk," he urged her. "There has got to be a plausible explanation that will satisfy others. The children can't keep saying they have a half brother who has no father whatsoever but who was apparently the product of a phantom of the night, someone who slipped in and out of your life in a manner of seconds and in the process fathered a child without equal, a mortal that doesn't fit in mortality, a child prodigy without equal, someone the substance of which cannot be measured by earthly terms."

"Surely they're not saying *that*."

"No, but that's the only recourse they have at present, although not in that same language, of course."

She was intently searching for the right answer. When none could be found, she spoke haltingly, "I'm still not sure there is an answer, dear. I know one thing, though, I will never say I was violated by another man. I won't say that because I would die first before that could happen, and I won't lie about what happened. That's not an option either."

"All right, Anne, I believe you. I believe you sincerely without question." He drew his handkerchief and wiped his suddenly moist face and eyes so that he could more clearly see and feel her grief exploding from within. Finally, he spoke, "Then we must tell them the truth, the absolute truth."

She wavered. "I'm not sure I know all there is to know about the actual event. That's why I've never said much. That and of course, because I know I won't be believed, and I don't want my son to become characterized as a child with no father, you know the term, and be mocked and joked about his entire life…"

"Anne, what do you think people are saying now? Don't you know that there are countless stories going around, speculation about who the father is, and what happened to precipitate the birth? We've got to say something that will bring an end to the speculation…"

"Isaac, are you sure?"

"I am. We must tell the children who Jesse's father is and trust God to do the rest. Tell me, please, what you remember of that night."

She thought back to the night fully seventeen years ago, when her life had been altered so completely beyond anything she had ever imagined, and wondered again how it had happened. "I remember the dream," she recounted, her words slipping out as if in a trance, "and I thought I talked with someone who appeared to me as someone divine—or listened rather—and he asked if I would be willing to be the mother of a very special child. I agreed because of the wonderous feeling that had overcome me, and he proceeded to tell me things that I must do to prepare myself for the birth. He said the way would be opened to make it possible." She stopped to take a deep breath. "Later, I found that I was pregnant... I had just become a teenager, only thirteen, and knew absolutely nothing about how babies are formed or of childbirth. I was as naïve as naïve could be, a baby myself if the truth were known. How can I explain that to my children when I can't even explain it to myself?"

He listened, absorbed in thought, comparing her comments to a dream he had experienced earlier, following the birth of the child, when it was conveyed to him uniquely that he should marry Anne despite the advent of the child and that it was acceptable that she hadn't broken any moral laws. Remembering that, he said reluctantly, "Then we must tell them the truth as it happened and trust that they will not ridicule what we say and accept it as the truth."

"Then we must tell them the truth, as it happened," he concluded, "and trust that they will not ridicule what we say and accept it as the truth."

"I'm not sure that's the right thing to do, Isaac," she persisted. "I'm afraid that would alienate others toward him. They would not only ridicule him, but they would attack him as a hypocrite, a blasphemer, as a hoax and liar. It would get ugly, I'm sure, and might even cost him his life..."

"But, Anne, if he is a son of someone like the Almighty himself, as you say, then he has to be known as such. The God of heaven has a purpose for him. It has to come out sooner or later so that he can do whatever it is he has been sent here to do."

"I suppose so."

He took time to weigh all the possibilities. "You're closer to the boy than I am, as his mother, has he ever said anything about his purpose here? Is he to become a king or a president even? Is he going to establish a creed of living, a church? Will he become recognized as a world leader? What's to become of him?"

She closed her eyes and thought back to the times when she and her son had talked personally. There were very few times at all, she realized.

"He hasn't said much," she confided, "hardly anything. I wonder just how much he knows presently anyway. I think he's still trying to determine the extent of his mission, whatever he is supposed to embrace. I believe that's why he spends so much time by himself, in solitude, trying to sort things out with his actual father."

"His father? Surely the time will come when it will all become transparent, for him and for us. What do we do until that time, Anne? I simply don't know what to say or do."

She suddenly felt a moment of strong conviction. "Then we must leave it for the present time and do the best we can to live with the situation and attempt to satisfy the questions that are becoming so overwhelming."

He clenched and unclenched his hands repeatedly then bowed his head then blinked hard, his chin set firmly and acquiesced. "Are you sure?"

"I am. It will come out soon enough, I feel strongly. We must let his actual father speak to him with the assurance that it will be what he needs to make his life take shape. We must be patient and let that happen according to God's time. The boy is doing the very best he can to make that happen. We have to allow it to happen at his own pace."

"And the children?"

She grabbed both his hands. "They must wait, along with us. They have a purpose in this as well. It will all come out, Isaac, in God's time."

"In God's time then…"

Chapter 3

James Encounters Bailey

JAMES AND BAILEY had sequestered themselves in his bedroom. Bailey and his sister, Mary Alice, enjoyed the privilege of having rooms to themselves in the handsome, old colonial-style home, which had been modernized, outside and in, an attractive face-lift being the singular feature of the spacious affair externally. The two boys were currently enjoying the distraction of a video as displayed on the television monitor with a rating of "R" for language and nudity.

"You ever see anything like that before?" Bailey questioned James.

"I've got sisters too," he answered tersely.

"Well, okay, but you haven't got sisters like that," he said, and he pointed out a specific highlight, in his eyes anyway.

"Maybe not but the idea is the same."

"The idea, yes, but it's what you can do with the idea that separates the men from the boys, my friend."

"I guess so."

"Listen, I can hook you up with someone who can help you overcome your timidity if you like. In fact, my sister—"

"Nah, I'm okay. I'll ease into dating as I get the urge. There's no sense rushing it, especially when I've got other things on my mind."

"Other things? What's more important than a healthy relationship with a girl? Something like that can set you up for life, prepare you for whatever you find in the big, cruel world we live in." The boy had a few pictures of attractive women on the walls, posing in skimpy bathing suits.

"They're pretty," he conceded, "if that's what you like."

"If that's what you like? Come on, don't tell me you don't come on to a beautiful girl—"

"Oh, I know when I see a beautiful girl all right, but I'm just saying the time isn't right for me at present. I'll know when the time is right, Bailey."

"All right, I'll quit bugging you, fella, but believe me, you don't know what you're missing. A man—and I do mean a man—was made for a woman."

"I agree with you, Bailey, but let's let it go at that, all right?" James didn't want to be pushed into anything, especially not now and not by a friend who obviously had license to do whatever he pleased, regardless of his age.

"All right, bud. Hey, help me understand what it is that turns you on. What is it about your family that makes everybody question just what it is that's going on?"

"What do you mean?"

"I mean, what about your older brother? People say weird things about him, like he was transplanted from another world and has no father, that he is a supernatural stud, an Einstein, or even more gifted, a god of some sort."

James laughed despite the absurdity. "He's human, believe me, but he is a little hard to live with sometimes."

"Like what? Help me understand. I've never seen the guy do anything that normal boys do, like play baseball or have dates, dance some crazy dance, get terribly excited."

"No, he doesn't show his emotions much, at least not for others. Although I think he feels emotions as strongly as anyone you'll meet."

"Does he laugh? Does he ever cry or lose his temper? I think the kid must have a screw loose somewhere. He's not normal, I tell you."

"Maybe not normal in the same sense that others are normal. He has his own way about doing things, but still, he's normal. He bleeds red blood, he cries at times—not often—but not usually because of what happens to him but for others because he seems to feel keenly the pains of others. I'm not sure you understand that. Mom keeps telling us that he's very precocious, you know what I mean. He's more mature than his actual age."

"That's a fact. I certainly agree with that, but it doesn't answer the question of where he came from. People say that Isaac isn't the father. Is that right?"

James was stumped. He didn't know what to say, even though he had reasoned with the question ever since he first found out that Jesse was a half brother. "I wish I knew" was all he could say.

"You mean you don't know whether he's your brother or not?" The boy was flabbergasted, his face flashing brightly in contrast with his raspberry-colored hair.

"Oh, I know he's a half brother all right, but I don't know any of the details."

Bailey was skeptical. "You don't know, or you're not saying? Come on, bud, you can level with me."

"No, I don't know, Bailey, I really don't, and I'm not sure my dad knows either."

"Oh, that's wild, man!"

"Yes, it is, but that's the way it is. They don't talk about it, and I probably shouldn't say anything either. So I guess I better shut my trap, except to say that Jesse is as normal as normal can be when you get to know him. He has different likes and dislikes than most, I agree, and keeps to himself a lot, but he is as true a friend or person as can be found anywhere. He loves others and will do anything for anybody if they need help. He's like that, a genuine good person, and that's all I'm going to say. Please don't ask me any more questions."

Bailey was quiet, introspective, analyzing the face of the other. Finally, he relented. "All right. I accept that. Let's see if we can have some fun tonight. Just the two of us, okay? Do you play cards? How 'bout some poker?"

"They're warm."

"What else?"

She hesitated, thinking more deeply about the physical contact they were sharing. "They're firm and strong. They're quite a bit larger than mine."

"Okay," he responded, "what does that tell you about the relationship between you and me?"

She took time to think seriously about his question. "It means, well, it means that you're older, more confident, more willing to help, more like a guiding light, I think, as long as the two of us retain that grip."

"That's absolutely right," he assured her. "That's the kind of relationship that you enjoy with your Heavenly Father. It can be called a spirit-to-spirit relationship, where you feel his presence guiding you. His spirit is his hand in yours."

"But does he speak?"

"Sometimes."

"Has he spoken to you?"

He looked more deeply into her eyes. "He has."

"And do you speak to him as well?"

"I do."

"Then you speak to each other?"

"We do."

"Can you tell me about it?"

"I can but it wouldn't mean much to you, not at this time, because it's personal stuff meant just for me at present. But in the same manner, he speaks to you as well."

"Oh, no, that's where you're wrong. He has never spoken to me." She broke the grip between the two of them.

He looked down at their hands, now separated, and reached for her hands again. "Do you feel my hands again?"

"Y-es, I do."

"That's God speaking to you, Jeri, as surely as the two of us are together with clenched hands, speaking to one another. What you must learn to do is to listen when he speaks so that you know what it is he is telling you."

"How can you be so sure?"

He smiled. "His hand is in mine, Jeri. I will never let go."

She felt a surge of anxiety overwhelm her and blurted out the words, "Do you know who your father is?"

"I do now," he answered. "There was a time when I didn't, when I was much younger."

"Have you met him then?"

He hesitated, apparently not sure how to reply.

"I'm sorry if I've offended you," she offered. "It's just that I'm curious. We're all curious, I guess you know."

"I know and it's all right. Actually, I know more than I can tell for the present, and so I'll just say that my father is not of this world, Jeri. He belongs to another world, similar to this one."

She was aghast. "Are you an alien then?"

"Aren't we all?" He smiled coyly, that infuriating little smile that always left others guessing what it was that he was suppressing.

"What do you mean, Jesse? Please tell me. I won't say anything to the others if you don't want me to."

"It's not what you think, Jeri." He took her hand in his again and squeezed gently. "I'm not explaining my situation in full because to do so would mean that others, especially family, would become targets for criticism from others, a good deal more than at present. Yes, I'm aware of what people are saying, but believe me, the criticism could become dangerous. Even worse, it could mean that those closest to me could lose their lives. I'm not ready to do that. I may never be ready. It's something I've got to deal with, that's all, and yes, I would prefer that you wouldn't say anything to the others."

Her cheery, red cheeks had brightened. Her short, puffy, brown hair with natural curls had become motionless, as had her face, lips parted in suspenseful silence. "Can you tell me anything more? I promise I won't say anything to the others."

He squeezed her hand again. "No, Jeri, I can't, even though I would love to tell you all that others only guess at now. I can only say that it will all come out eventually and that you will play a part for me and for God. Keep searching for that identity with God, and

I promise you that the answers you seek will come from him and not from me."

"From him, from God?"

"Yes." And he caressed her hand and let go. "From God, especially for you."

She was relieved somewhat but downcast. "Can you tell me if you were joking when you said that we're aliens? You weren't serious, were you?"

"Oh, but I was, Jeri. It's something you'll learn from God as well. I'll just say that none of us is native to this world, Black or White or otherwise. We've all had a beginning elsewhere and leave it at that."

"Boy, I've got a lot of learning to do," she exploded, "and now I've got to find God so that I can get the answers. Anything else?" she added, her hopelessness spewing out with each uttered word.

"No, that's all for now. It will come, Jeri. I promise you. Let it come at God's own time and don't press too much. That won't help."

"All right, Jesse, but I'm more bewildered now than I was before. Can you just tell me one thing?"

"What is it, Jeri?"

"Are you my real brother? I love you with all my heart and want to know."

He took her in his arms and cradled her tightly as he fought to control his emotions. "Yes, Jeri, I'm your real brother, and you're my real sister forever, in God's plan for families."

"Thank you, Jesse. You've made me very happy."

Chapter 5

A Complex Chain of Events

JERROD HOUSTON WAS a self-made man. More than that, he was also a self-proclaimed individual in that he harbored great feelings for himself and his enterprise to the exclusion of others, especially competitors. He was the GM of Houston-Barrett Construction, a huge construction company that had within the past year moved its headquarters to the suburbs of a major eastern city, expecting that the growth in that giant metropolis would flood the suburbs and allow for a bonanza in expected income.

Fifty years old and laced with an impressive array of stern looks and time-worn principles to match, he loved competition and, together with his silent partner, multimillionaire Ted Barrett, had invested a huge amount of money in the move to capture the construction industry as it moved into the suburbs before others could imagine what the future would hold for such a bold move.

The problem: there was going to be some lag time before the expected crescendo happened, and now the company was sitting and waiting impatiently while the major source of their plan-ahead capital had begun to grow restless, waiting for a return on a prodigious loan, a loan that had included enough hard money to keep three separate crews and their respective foremen busy, along with keeping up with contractual payments for the use of heavy equipment and their operators, a lofty expense as well but necessary since such equipment was needed in meeting deadlines promised under contract.

There was another problem, too, that was particularly vexing to Jerrod Houston, the man who loved a fight because he always won in the end, and that problem involved amazingly a one-man construction company by the name of Isaac, a custom builder. That company with a payroll of only one person, Isaac himself, currently had a stranglehold on local construction activity. The man had been around for several years and was noted for high quality and fair pricing in an otherwise unscrupulous industry, one that was now laced with inflated pricing suddenly ruled by fortune hunters, high-rollers who were pushing prices of materials out of sight in due partly to the fact that industry—all industry—had become controlled with unions and computer-driven technology and corporate levels of management to the point that the average person or family or small business couldn't begin to use their services so overpriced were they.

Jerrod Houston had grasped the problem and was busy planning how to eliminate the competition without having to simply blast the man into smithereens along with his skill set so outdated and orthodox that it reeked of simplicity and honest labor, a thing of the past. For that reason, he had asked his son, Bailey, to become friendly with one of Isaac's sons, James, and learn more about the family. He had heard things about the family that were highly irregular and, considering those things, wondered if he couldn't start a smear campaign against the family that would inevitably put Isaac Christian, custom builder, out of business.

In ultracompetitive high business circles, a move such as this would be tame, he knew. Most uncompromising GMs would simply offer a settlement to such an individual and, if he didn't accept, hire a strong-armed undercover operator to convince him or her that it was time to retire or seek another source of employment, or else. A smear campaign would take a little time to unfold, but it would work without having to resort to any nasty covertness. In the meantime, he would have to find a way to pacify his silent partner, Ted Barrett, who had stuck his neck out a good deal more than he originally planned in order to secure financing the move, involving more than one major loan institutions, he wasn't sure just how many, to be sure.

With a plan in mind, he had asked his son to find out whatever he could about the family. "Invite the boy, James, to come over," he had told Bailey, "and see what you can find out that can be useful later, anything of an irregular nature, you understand?"

"I think so, Dad," the boy had replied, not sure what his father had in mind.

"Well, there's this gossip about the boy's brother, Jesse, I think they call him. I've heard that he's illegitimate, that the mother had an affair with someone else. I need to know the particulars if you can find out," he had continued.

"Okay, Dad," he had replied, still not sure just where all this was heading.

"That will be a start," his father had offered, and the boy knew he had a job to do or else suffer the consequences.

He had failed his father before and didn't want that to happen again, knowing firsthand of the relentless nature of his father. The man was not someone to be trifled with. His mother had made that point vivid enough several times in fact, and he had felt the force of his father's disappointment in a harsh manner as well and had the bruises to show for it.

Later, following the overnight visit of James with Bailey, the father made it a point to get with his son and find out what had transpired that might be useful in beginning his smear campaign against Isaac Christian and his one-man construction company that was effectively stifling one of the truly great and powerful construction dynamos of its time, Houston-Barrett Construction. The conversation went something like this as they met alone in the expansive living room of the home after the man had suggested firmly that the boy turn off his iPhone so that it wouldn't be a disturbance:

"Son, were you able to find out anything irregular about James and the family, particularly about his brother, the illegitimate one?"

The boy was fidgeting, knowing he had failed his father. "No, Dad, I didn't."

"What do you mean you didn't? Did you question him at all?"

"I did, Dad, but he didn't say much."

"What did he say? Did you make it a point to press him on the matter?"

"What do you mean, Dad?"

"I mean, did you try and force the issue a little, or did you just say, 'How are things going?' and call it good?"

"I asked a few questions, Dad. He really didn't want to talk about his brother, though."

The man was perplexed and let it be known that the boy had certainly let him down, his gruff nature coming quickly to the surface, cuffing the boy lightly on the ear. "Tell me what he said when you asked him about his brother," he demanded, "word for word."

The boy thought for a moment, his face screwed up in indecision before spitting out his reply: "He told me the boy is normal, that he bleeds like others and that he has likes and dislikes just like others." And he added quickly, "He also said that his brother cares for others, a lot. I think that was it."

"Oh, boy, you really did a bang-up job, didn't you?"

"I'm sorry, Dad. I did the best I could."

"Okay, son. Let's leave it at that. The next time, though, see if you can't put a little more effort into doing what I asked you to do. You understand?"

"Yes, Dad. I will. I promise."

Chapter 6

Jesse and His Father Together

JESSE WAS AWAY from home for a few days, something he hadn't done before. Usually, when he left to be by himself, it was only for hours at a time. This time, inexplicably, he was gone for four days, and when he finally came back from his solitary retreat, Anne and Isaac were highly animated. It was the first time the others, including James, had seen his mother scold Big Brother, who seemed to take it in stride, silently absorbing the censuring.

When he finally spoke, it was without a semblance of an excuse: "There are things that I must figure out for myself, Mother. I can't do that unless I work at it in my own way."

"But, son," she remonstrated, "we had no idea whether you were alive or dead. You must consider Isaac and myself when you leave without giving us a hint of how long you intend to be gone. We were so anxious. You could have been in a terrible way, and we wouldn't have even known where you were or what you were doing. We've had the police looking for you. Now we've got to call them and say it was all a misunderstanding—"

"Yes," he replied slowly, "and I understand how it seems to you and to Isaac. I will try to do better. I didn't intend to be gone so long. The time slipped away…"

"What have you been doing for meals, son?" she pressed further. "Did you take anything with you?"

He looked at the others who had gathered around by this time, anxious to know of his absence. It was dark and close to bedtime. The younger children, especially crowded close, soothed in part by his calm voice and demeanor.

He paused long enough to hug nine-year-old Jana and replied, "I did not. I didn't think to prepare myself in that way."

"Did you have any water, son?"

He responded by tilting his head perceptibly from side to side and uttered, "I had what I needed, Mother. That was sufficient."

"You must be starving, son. Please, sit down and I'll prepare something for you to eat."

"It's not necessary, Mother. I'll eat in the morning with the others."

"But, Jesse, you can't live on nothing at all!" She was clearly exasperated, her motherly instincts taking control of the situation. She turned to go to the area of the house that included the pantry and eating quarters.

"Mother," he stopped her short, a hand on her shoulder. "I'm all right. I've been with my father."

The others stared at him as if he had just risen from the dead, mouths agape, eyes wide, frozen in motion, considering the words that had just been spoken.

"All right, son," she managed to say, meekly aware of what had just been revealed.

Her son was beginning a new chapter in his life. Just where it would end, she couldn't say, but her whole body trembled at the thought of how it would involve each of them in turn for good and for bad in the extreme. She would not sleep tonight. Sleep—pure, unadulterated sleep—such as she had known in her more youthful years would never come again, she feared.

Chapter 7

An Ideological Difference

AT THE START of the next workday, a Monday, Isaac asked Jesse to help him begin work on a four-bedroom home he had contracted to build for a family new to the community. The head of the family, a man with impressive credentials in engineering circles, was relatively unknown locally but figured chiefly in plans to develop a hydroelectric generating station nearby, at the confluence of two major rivers, a potential bonanza for power that would be needed as the community continued to grow.

After carefully studying blueprints for the dwelling to be constructed, Isaac had used his transit to measure distances and set the necessary stakes for the corners upon which the concrete footing would be laid, preliminary to the stem or support system for the home itself. He was attaching strong yellow twine to the stakes, marking the line to be followed while digging the footing, and establishing the depth of the ditch that would follow when he was suddenly accosted by a large figure of a man dressed in an impressive-looking tailored dark suit and tie. The man's shiny Florsheim shoes were showing dust as he had picked his way through the dirt, where he and Jesse were finishing up the necessary outline they were to follow while digging. His large silver belt buckle gleamed brightly.

"Hello there," the man said, offering his right hand to Isaac without smiling, "I'm Jerrod Houston of Houston-Barrett Construction. Maybe you've heard of me."

"I have," Isaac replied and took the other's hand in a firm handshake that lingered a bit too long. "I'm Isaac Christian and this is Jesse," pointing to his foster son. "What can we do for you?"

The man paused to look around at what had been done in preparing the lot upon which the two individuals would be working and replied, "You sure go about this in a strange way."

"Yes…" he replied, getting a feel for what the man would say next.

"You know they've got machines that can do the work for you now and save a great deal of manual labor. That is, if you want to expedite things in your construction business." The man continued to look critically at the setup and screwed up his face in displeasure. "Have you ever heard of a Ditch Witch?"

"Oh, yes, I've heard of the little ditching machine that makes short work out of digging the footing. Why do you ask?"

"Well, because it could save you a lot of work, you know, and time. In my business time is money, and that makes a lot of difference in the long run when you're considering profit and loss."

"I understand," he replied noncommittal, nodding in agreement.

The man studied his face before continuing, "Then why don't you use one, instead of working yourself to death with a shovel?"

Isaac thought briefly of the question, peering at the man's bronzed face covered in part by a white Stetson hat that looked to be made of 100 percent pure beaver fur, and answered, "Because I like to feel the soil around which I'm going to build the home."

"*Feel the soil?* I don't understand. How can that possibly be of benefit in the long run other than to stall the development of the building itself?"

Isaac grimaced. "No, you probably wouldn't."

The man continued, "I mean, if you don't want to put a lot of money into a ditching machine, you can always rent one. Surely you can afford that?"

"I can." He closed his eyes and nodded again.

"Then why don't you use one? Are you in the business to make money, or is this just a tax dodge or something you do for fun?"

Isaac smiled and glanced at Jesse, who was intently taking note of the interaction between the two men. "Money is all right," he answered quietly, "but it's not the most important part of the contractual agreement between two individuals as far as I'm concerned."

"So what's more important than making a profit?"

Isaac didn't hesitate any longer, speaking directly toward the man, "I believe integrity is the most important thing in any agreement. I agree to build a home and do so without cutting cost or labor, using quality materials and workmanship. That's the way I work, and I expect the same from anyone who works for me. When I get paid for my work, I expect full payment because I know I've done the best job that I possibly can and earned every cent of the agreed price."

The man was clearly baffled. "So how does digging a ditch by hand rather than using a machine rate as the preferred method of completing the footing?" And he gestured toward the outline set off by stakes and twine.

Isaac took a deep breath and let it out. "Sir," he began, "when I dig the footing, I note the composition of the soil, whether it's alkaline, sandy, or rocky, to a fault, or otherwise. I determine which part of the footing might be most prone to settle and thereby needs reinforcing. I carefully note the soluble content of the soil, whether it has been immersed to the point of becoming badly saturated, and thereby unstable. When you come right down to it, the foundation of the building is the most integral part of the building, determining how long the structure will last over time. Do you understand now?"

The man carefully considered the statement of the other. "Yes," he said finally. "I do and I have to agree with you. I have something to add if you will listen, and I hope you do so, for your sake."

"What is it?"

"I would like to offer you a job as a construction foreman, and you can name your salary. What do you say?"

Isaac didn't hesitate: "Sir, I can't work for you."

"Why not? Is it that money thing again?"

"No, it has nothing to do with money."

"Then what is it?"

Isaac took note of the other's demeanor, how it had suddenly changed. He started to turn away and resume work.

The man grabbed his shoulder and turned him around, facing him with a grim, defiant face. "What is it? I asked."

He couldn't hold back the words: "It has something to do with integrity. When I work for someone, I do so because I believe that man has the same work ethic that I do. I won't compromise, sir." And he stood his ground, unblinking.

"Okay," the man said, "I understand." He deliberated for a moment before starting again. "What if we buy you out, would that work? You can name your price, within reason, but I warn you, if you don't accept, we'll run right over the top of you. You won't have a leg to stand on when we're through, and that's a promise. Now you think seriously about it because I need an answer, and it needs to come by tomorrow. I won't wait any longer. What do you say?"

Isaac stiffened. "You don't have to wait, sir, the answer is no, not at any price."

The man was clearly outraged. He turned and bolted toward his big black Cadillac, his Florsheim shoes turning up the dust.

"We haven't seen the last of that one," Jesse commented.

"I'm afraid you're right. What would your father tell you to do, in this situation?" he questioned, wondering about the boy's answer.

Jesse didn't flinch. "I'd like to think that he would tell you not to lessen yourself by merging with or doing business with Houston-Barrett Construction Company. Instead, he'd say you've worked hard to build up your reputation as a custom builder, a builder of fine homes, every home a palace fit for a king and queen. That's what I imagine he would say, and I certainly agree."

"And the consequence?"

"He'd say, 'Put your trust in me, and I'll make the difference.'"

"All right. Here we go, you and me and your father."

Chapter 8

Jesse's Future Takes Shape

ANNE COULDN'T WAIT to catch Jesse alone so that she could draw him out about his time spent with his "*father*," as he had termed it. The chance finally came to her a couple of days later, after he had come home from working with Isaac at the new construction site. He was tired and had sat down to rest a moment before resuming his activities for the day.

"Are you going to shower?" she asked, beginning the conversation.

"Maybe later. I think I'll study for a while first as soon as I catch my breath. Dad (meaning Isaac) worked me pretty hard."

"Oh, how are things going at the site?" She felt a reluctance to begin, hoping he might refer to the incident with his father himself voluntarily.

"All right, except that we had quite an experience Monday with a man who operates a new construction company in our area."

"Yes, he told me about that. I'm worried that the man will cause some problems, aren't you?"

"He could. Apparently, his company is big-time stuff, and he doesn't want any competition, especially not from Dad."

"That is scary, isn't it? Do you have anything else that's been bothering you, son?"

"What do you mean?"

"I mean, well, anything that you feel like you need to talk to me about?" She was about to give up and force the conversation to her initial interest.

He sat up and adjusted a couch pillow behind his back, a hint of a smile playing on his lips, before speaking. "I'm sorry, Mom, that I haven't been more explicit about my meeting with *Father* last week. I'm sure that's what you would like to talk about, isn't it?"

"Yes, son, it is." She sat down beside him and put her arm around him and squeezed. "I have a right to know, don't I?"

"You do, and I've been thinking about the best way to discuss it without alarming you and without any kind of misrepresentation on my part, as the incident occurred."

"I'm not sure I understand. You mean you want to be truthful but not hurt my feelings?"

"I guess that's it, yes."

"Why should I have my feelings hurt, son? You know I have nothing but the greatest love and concern for you."

"Yes, of course, but I don't want you to think that you are being belittled in any way by being left out of the experience."

"Son"—she hugged him tightly—"I know you have a mission in this life. I know that with all my heart. I know I can be a part of that mission through you and that I'm privileged to share it in a special way as your mother. You can't offend me by seeking to know your part in that mission, only if you choose to ignore me and not include me in your progress and plans." She reached over and kissed him on the cheek.

"I understand, Mother."

"There are probably things that happened that you can't tell me, but I'm hoping that I can share in the experience in some ways. Is that all right?"

"Yes." He closed his eyes and pursed his lips together, recalling the glorious moments together with the man called *Father*. "First of all," he began, "I'm not ready for my calling, or mission, as you referred to it. I'm going to be staying at home for a while, possibly several years, I'm not sure exactly."

"Did he tell you that?"

"Yes, he did, and he also told me that I need to do more studying and praying to prepare myself for that time when I will go forth."

"*Go forth?* What does that mean?"

He closed his eyes again and looked up, as if seeing the vision again. "It means that I will become a messenger for God throughout the world."

"Throughout the world? What kind of messenger, son?"

He raised his arms to chest level and spread his hands open, palms upturned. "It means that I'm going to share some of God's revealed truths to the world. It's going to be a glorious mission, Mother, but I can't reveal at this time what those revealed truths will be. In fact, I don't know what they are completely. I have only a glimpse at this time, nothing more, but I must continue to prepare myself for those truths to be revealed in full."

"I see." She reflected on how that mission might reflect upon others as well before inquiring, "Will you marry, son? Will you have a family?"

He lowered his head in thought. "I don't believe so, Mother. Nothing was said about having a family, not in the present anyway."

"What do you mean by *present?* Is there a chance that a family might be in the future then?"

"I believe so. Nothing was said about that, however. I must concentrate on gaining knowledge. '*Knowledge is power,*' I was told. As I gain more knowledge, I gain more power to the point that I can represent God in my travels."

"You mean, you might be able to perform some miracles in God's name?"

"Yes, even so if I do it for God's sake, not to promote myself, not to pretend that I'm God himself in any manner."

"Of course." His comment striking home, she asked: "How will you gain godly knowledge other than through study and prayer? Did *Father* offer any other manner of learning about becoming godly?"

He pondered the question then replied, "He did, yes, and this is where I need to be careful."

"*Careful?* In what way, son?"

He fought to control his emotions, his voice constricted in his throat. "He told me that if I remained vigilant and didn't give in to the ways of the world, if I sought to know with all my heart, that others would come and instruct me in all that I needed to know, including himself…"

"You're to have teachers then?"

"Yes, teachers, or mentors, from heaven. It's going to be a glorious opportunity to learn from angels and more in the same manner in which I've been receiving help already. I think you know about that, not with personal contact but with thought interaction, a spirit-to-spirit thing."

"Son, I couldn't be happier for you. Please tell me, will you continue to help Isaac in his work? He needs you."

"I will, for the present anyway. There will come a time, however, when I will have to leave for good."

She couldn't hold back a tear. "I understand, son." She started to stand then thought of another question, something that had been on her mind a lot lately. "Son, will your mission be dangerous to yourself or to others? Will you become a martyr for God, like so many others who have given themselves to be prophets and the like?"

He started to speak then held back before relenting. "It's something I can't speak about now, Mother. I don't know all the things about my mission, only what is pertinent to know at present, but I have been told that I must prepare myself for difficulties that will come, perhaps of a tragic nature that affect others, even family. I don't know all there is to know about that aspect."

A silence followed, broken only by her subliminal fears and muffled attempts to clear her eyes so badly misted over.

Chapter 9

Mary Alice Enters the Picture

JERROD HOUSTON WAS, anyone who knew him would say, a man of action. Isaac Christian, the custom builder, had run over the top of him with the notion that he wasn't a man of integrity, and therefore the two of them couldn't do business together. Okay, he was about to teach a lesson to the man concerning integrity. Integrity, to him, meant that when he was cornered, he would fight back; when faced with a challenge, he would do all that was necessary to overcome whatever odds were against him and come out on top. That was integrity, the Jerrod Houston way. It meant you can count on me when things are tight. When the going gets rough, I won't quit, and I won't run out on my partner either.

It was time to call in the first team. He had asked his son, Bailey, to gather information about Isaac and his family, especially the peculiar one, Jesse, so that he could begin his smear program and successfully run the man out of business. That hadn't produced the results he was looking for. He was confident, however, that his backup plan would succeed.

The backup involved Bailey's older sister, Mary Alice, two years the boy's senior, the oldest of his and his wife's two children. Mary Alice, the kids would say, was hot; in other words, she was quite a number. That she was a little more than either he or his wife, Sally, could handle was also true. The girl was petulant, sassy at times, and

downright incorrigible; but when needed, she could also be allur-
ing, charming, and even seductive in an overpowering manner. She
had all the equipment that was needed, including long dark hair,
beautifully amplified over her exquisitely contoured face and neck
areas, dark, brooding eyes with powerful mystique that screamed to
be adored, and the figure of a fashion model. In short, she was a diva,
a prima donna, a girl well fitted to turn any man upside down and
land him wherever she wanted, mostly in the palm of her hand. She
could bewitch them and then laugh about the conquest and often
did. That was his daughter. She was one in a million, and he freely
admitted that neither he nor his wife could do anything to stop her.
She was a one-woman wrecking crew, perfectly suited to do his job
for him and never look back.

The challenge: Get Mary Alice with Jesse and find out if the guy
was human or not. That meant that he would have to go through the
boy's younger brother, James, using Bailey, as before, a go-between,
and arrange a meeting between Jesse and Mary Alice. That meeting would be like Superman walking into a room filled with kryp-
tonite, his Waterloo, his undoing, regardless of where he came from
or what his magical powers happened to be; it was Delilah cutting off
Samson's hairy locks, rendering him useless; it was the *Titanic* going
down in the north Atlantic with 1,517 casualties. It was just plain
brilliant, and his daughter was the perfect one for the job.

He wasted no time finding Bailey and explaining his part in the
drama. The boy was still friends with James, Jesse's younger brother,
and wouldn't mess this one up, he was sure. It had to be done right,
though. James had to be convinced that Mary Alice was genuinely
interested in Jesse, was sweet on him, and wanted a chance to grow
that relationship. If done in that manner, he was sure that the plan
would succeed. James would then set up a meeting between the two
older siblings. That would begin what would surely be a fatal attrac-
tion. No one could say no to Mary Alice; no one that was human,
that was.

Once the relationship between Mary Alice and Jesse was established, he felt sure that he would be able to learn enough about the
boy as well as the family to begin his smear campaign in earnest. He

would begin by publicizing the illegitimacy of the boy, emphasizing how the family had protected the youth by keeping knowledge of his father in strictest confidence, indicating to others who wished to know of the personal nature of the father that the man was obviously a convict or a common thief, someone of a fly-by-night nature, here today and gone tomorrow, perhaps in prison at the present time. That would reflect horribly upon the family and surely lead to a large-scale boycott of Christian's business interest in the community, opening the door for Houston-Barrett Construction to take over.

Settled in his mind about how he would proceed, he mentioned some of the bare facts of his plan to his wife, Sally, the next morning, before he left to go to work.

He was surprised at her reaction: "So you're going to throw your daughter at this boy and ask her to go to bed with him so that you can accuse him or rape or worse?"

"Heavens no, Sally! I have no intention of suggesting that Mary Alice do such a thing. Just who do you think I am anyway, a man with no consideration for my daughter at all?"

"Well, pardon me, but it sure sounds like it to me from what you've said."

He was dressed for work at the office in one of his regular tailor-made suits, and she was still in her lounge-around clothes, not planning to leave the house. The children had already left for school.

"I will do no such thing!" he blared out over her displeasure. "I'm simply doing what I feel is necessary in order to establish ourselves in this community. If I don't do something quickly, the company will most likely have to declare bankruptcy. How would that suit you and your card-playing group—the Bridge Forum, I think you call yourselves—that sit and berate anyone who isn't invited and spend money like it fell out of the sky?"

She was stunned by his comment, and recognizing the tone of his voice and how dangerously she was treading on thin ice, she spoke more sympathetically, "Well, do what you feel you have to do, but please be understanding of Mary Alice's feelings too. She may not want anything to do with that strange boy."

He consented with a nod of his head. "I'll be careful, you can be sure of that. I'm not going to put our daughter in any danger at all. I'm only asking her to find out a few things about the family that need to be said in order to allow Houston-Barrett Construction to assume control of the construction industry in this area."

"Okay, Jerrod, you have my studied approval, I guess. After all, I'd really like to know more about that family too. They seem so proper and perfect. Yet we all know there's more going on than meets the eye, and it should come out, shouldn't it?"

Chapter 10

The Soap Opera Begins

JERROD HOUSTON RECEIVED a minor setback when he first talked of his plan with his daughter, Mary Alice.

"You want me to do *what?*" she asked, not sure she had heard correctly, her portraiture-perfect youthful face masked in uncertainty and disdain.

He halted, trying not to show his lack of patience and, squaring his shoulders, replied, "I want you to make an effort to get to know Jesse Christian, James' older brother, so that I can get information about the family."

"Why, Dad?" She was dressed in holy—make that holey—Levi's and a sloppy sweatshirt. The Levi's were so holey that there wasn't much fabric left for viewing but a lot of skin.

"I have my reasons," he shot back, "and it's important. That's all you need to know."

"But, Dad," she argued, "the boy is a weirdo from what I've been told. He doesn't mix with others. He doesn't even mix with his own family. The kids are all wondering where he came from, according to what Bailey said. I don't want anything to do with him."

"Have you met the boy?"

"No, and let's leave it at that, okay? I've got better things to do than chase after the *Phantom of the Opera* or whatever he is."

He didn't want to have to tell her all of his plan, especially that she was key to success if it were to work, and quickly mellowed. "Dearie..." he began.

"You never call me that, Dad, unless you're frantic or your head's on the chopping block."

"Don't be cute, Mary Alice, and yes, I need your help. I need it in the worst way, okay?"

"All right, Dad, but it's going to cost you, you know that, don't you?"

He could sense success was in his grasp. "All right, what do you need this time?"

She smiled cutely, along with a hiccup of a laugh, exploding at the same time. "I really need a car, Dad, something I can drive next year when I go away to school."

He nodded, relieved that she didn't want the equivalent of the Taj Mahal or something similar. "I think we can work that out, honey," he offered.

"No! No maybe so, Dad! I need a car, a good one and not a used car either. It's needs to be a new one, sporty, and red, but I'll pick it out, okay?"

"Okay, sweetie, you'll get your car, the one you want."

"Boy, you're laying it on thick, Dad. You must really need the kid's life story. What if I can't deliver?"

"Oh, you'll deliver all right." He smiled knowingly. "There isn't a person alive who can say no to you when you're at your best. We both know that."

"All right, Dad. Now what is it I need to find out about this clod named Jesse?"

* * * * *

As it turned out, James had problems of his own after first meeting with Bailey, having been given the information that Mary Alice wanted to meet with Jesse, that she was personally interested....

During the ensuing meeting between James and Jesse, Jesse's reaction was "Who's Mary Alice, and why does she think she wants to meet with me? Say that again, please, James."

"I think she likes you, Jesse. She wants to get to know you better."

"But I've never met the girl. How could she possibly want to get to know me better?"

"I don't know, Jesse. Maybe she learned about you from her brother, Bailey. Anyway, she wants to meet. What do you say?"

He ran his fingers through his hair, perplexed. "Have you spoken to Bailey about me at all, James?"

"Only a little."

"What have you said?"

He hid his face behind his raised hand, trying to hide his indecision. "Just that you're a swell person, someone who is quite solitary, except when you work with Dad, and that we're not sure about your father."

"You've talked about my father?"

"Well, yes, only that we don't know anything about the man, whoever he is."

"And what was Bailey's reaction?"

"His reaction? Well, probably the same as ours. We're all curious about your father, you understand. No one seems to know much about it, including Mom and Dad, or at least, they're not saying."

He nodded before commenting, "I don't know much about it either."

"Oh, that's wild, man! Are you saying that you don't know much about your birth?"

"That's right, James. It's as much a mystery to me as it is to you. I couldn't begin to tell you how it happened, only that I accept that I've got a different father than you and the other children."

"And that you've met him?"

"Oh, yes, I've met him all right, and that's as much as I can say right now. At some time, perhaps in the not-too-distant future, I'll be able to say more, but that time hasn't come yet. Anyway, let's drop that subject, okay, and go back to Mary Alice. I really don't want to meet her, James, and it's not because I don't think she would be interesting or anything like that. But it's because I'm busy trying to do all I can right now to get ready for the time when I'll be leaving. I've got a lot to do before I can leave, and honestly, I don't have time to make close friends with anybody, not now anyway."

"Okay, I'll tell him. He'll be very disappointed, though, Jesse, and so will she."

What happened after that defies the imagination; it was bizarre, totally spontaneous, and as it turned out, life-changing: Jesse found time the next afternoon to walk to the construction site. The walls of the building were beginning to take shape, Jesse and Isaac having worked on the outside perimeter earlier. Isaac had made it plain to him that time spent helping with the framing would be greatly appreciated. It was to be a two-story affair with a large balcony and presented quite a challenge for one person.

A block away from the site, just past where the US Geological Survey station was housed with the local post office, he saw three girls beating up another girl on the sidewalk. They were trying to muscle the girl toward a nearby alleyway where they could finish the job. The girl's face was noticeably bloodied, and she was limp from the beating she had taken.

Jesse ran toward the melee, shouting at the girls. At first they disregarded him, anxious to finish the job, but when he started forcibly pushing the girls away, threatening to call the police, they bolted and left the scene.

The girl was a mess. He wasn't sure if she needed hospital attention or not but, taking out his handkerchief, started cleaning off her face. "You've got a bad nosebleed," he informed her, pinching off the blood. "Are there any broken bones?" he asked solicitously, realizing as he did so that she was in no condition to answer.

Without warning, she nearly fainted, and he held her securely until she could open her eyes.

"I've got you," he assured her, firmly supporting her weight.

Her eyes slowly came into focus. "I think I'm all right," she blubbered, "except for my ego, and that's shot."

When she was able to stand, he placed his arm around her waist and helped her limp slowly out of the entrance of the alleyway.

"There's water nearby," he told her, and when she began to stumble badly, he reached out and caught her and carried her to the construction site.

Isaac saw them coming and cleared off a place along the sub-flooring of the project where Jesse could set her down, resting her on his jacket that had been hanging on a wall stud close by. He then found a clean cloth in his service truck and moistened it with water from the outside hydrant, newly installed, and the two men gave assistance in washing off her face and arms where most of the blood had now dried.

After a few minutes, she mustered enough strength sit up and talk intelligently, offering her thanks for help received, adding: "I'm new to this area. I guess I was drawing too much attention from the boys, and those girls took it upon themselves to rearrange my face or else fit me for a coffin. I'm not sure which, maybe both. Anyway—" she sighed and wiped at her face, still smarting badly, puffy and bruised—"they did a good job. I'm glad you came along when you did." She turned to face Jesse, squinting visibly. "If you hadn't, my face would be hamburger now or maybe chop suey. I guess I owe you more than a thanks."

"You're going to be all right," Jesse assured her, "as long as you can avoid that bunch."

Now that she was partially cleaned up, he was suddenly aware that the girl was lovely, as lovely as anyone he'd ever seen without exception, notwithstanding the purple blotches and puffiness. It was hard not to blush as he stared at her.

She asked about her purse, and Jesse, recognizing that he hadn't seen it, got up and ran back to the place where she had been accosted and found it alongside the street and brought it back. She then pro-duced a cell phone and called her mother and told her what had happened.

"She's coming to get me," she offered. "I walked to the post office, something I do each morning for exercise, checking mail for my dad. He's the head of a construction group new to this area."

"That would be Houston-Barrett Construction?" Isaac questioned.

"Yes."

"And you would be Mary Alice?" Jesse concluded.

"Yes, how did you know?"

"I'm Jesse Christian," he informed her. "I think you wanted to meet me."

"*Oh no!*" she squealed loudly, covering her face with her hands. "*I'm chopped liver! I'll never live this down.*"

Chapter 11

Chopped Liver and Chopped Onions?

AFTER MARY ALICE'S mother arrived and forced pleasantries had been exchanged along with a quick explanation of what had transpired, Jesse and Isaac were left to muse about what had just taken place.

"You were fortunate to be able to help that girl," Isaac commented feelingly. "She could have been messed up badly."

He agreed, still thinking about the coincidence that had brought them together.

"You remember what her father said to us the morning we met him here?"

"Oh, yes. He was quite vocal."

"He's not going to like what happened today."

"No, but we didn't have anything to do with the attack on his daughter."

"Certainly not, but for him, as upset as he was, it may not make any difference. In fact, he may hold it against us."

"Why do you say that?"

"Well, as explosive as he appeared that morning, he may take it as an insult that we got involved at all."

THE SONG OF JESSE

"He might, Dad, but I don't think so. If he loves that girl, he will thank us for doing what we did for her, circumstances being what they were."

"I hope you're right. He strikes me as being quite irrational when he's pressed badly."

The following day, after Jesse and Isaac had returned from the construction site, there was a knock on the front door. Jeri answered and, after a short pause, called for Jesse to come to the door. It was Mary Alice, dressed smartly in a calico dress, white with yellow polka dots, and straps over the shoulders. Her face was still red and puffy, and a couple of small Band-Aids were spaced along the mouth and cheek.

She was blushing as she spoke. "I brought you and the others some chocolate chip cookies," she volunteered apologetically. "I hope you'll take them as thanks for helping me yesterday."

"That is sweet of you," he answered, taking the basket covered with red cloth. "They smell great."

"They're still warm," she volunteered. "They're best that way."

"Would you like to come in?" he questioned, opening the door wider and gesturing with a sweep of his arm.

"I would but I've really got to go. Can I come back some other time, though?" She added, "When I'm feeling better?" She blushed again, pointing at her face.

"Yes, certainly."

As she turned to go, Jesse handed the cookies off to Jeri and followed the girl outside. "Are you not feeling well then?" he questioned.

She stopped and smiled, meeting his stare, focused on her face. "I'm going to be all right, but I'm having some dizzy spells today. I hope they go away soon."

"Yes, of course." There was an awkward silence before he spoke again. "What are you going to do about those girls? I've got a feeling they may not be done with you."

"I'm not sure really. My mom wants to call the police and press charges. I don't want it to go that far, though. I think I can still make friends with the girls if they'll give me a chance."

"Be careful."

"I will." She backed away a step, preparing to turn and leave.

"What if," he proposed suddenly, "I walk with you when you go to the post office. Would that be all right?"

She peered at him intently. "You would be willing to do that for me?"

"Yes, I believe I can do that each morning as I go to work or whenever I'm available. I don't think you should be walking alone, at least not until you can make friends with those girls."

She smiled brightly, wincing as she did so because of the induced pain. "I would appreciate that a lot, Jesse." And she reached out and grasped his hand innocently.

Jesse smiled in return. "We can make quite a pair," he commented. "You and me. You'll be chopped liver and I'll be chopped onions."

"Oh, please don't make me laugh anymore," she forced out painfully.

After she left, James wasted no time cornering Jesse. "I thought you said you weren't interested in getting to know Mary Alice?"

"I didn't say I wasn't interested in getting to know her, James. I just said I was busy right now and didn't want to take time out to make new friends."

"Oh, I see, and so now you've decided that you have more time and can make new friends?"

He smiled half-heartedly. "Something like that, I guess. We were sort of thrown together, James. She didn't mean for it to happen and neither did I. It just happened. Now since I've gotten involved, I hate to just drop the whole affair as if it didn't happen. The girl needs some help, and yes, I'm busy. But I can still find a little time to help her. All right?"

"It's all right with me but be careful, she's got a reputation from what I've heard."

"A reputation for what?"

He searched for the right words without being too direct. "She comes on to men, or boys, whatever the case may be, and she likes to love them and then leave them, or the opposite too, is what I've heard. I'm not surprised that the other girls jumped her."

"Well, thanks for the warning, little brother. I'll be careful."

"I just know that this is your first taste of boy-meets-girl-type thing. I don't want you to get burned."

Jesse laughed. "And you're the expert in these matters?"

"I'm no expert, except that I've been told that love is blind. I think that may be true in this case. Mary Alice is a knockout. It's hard to see past the shine. I trust your judgment in most cases, but in things of the heart, with girls like Mary Alice, I'm not so sure you can't be fooled."

"Thanks, James. I know you wouldn't say anything unless you felt deeply that it needed to be said. I'll keep that in mind, I promise."

"One other thing," he persisted. "Bailey, Mary Alice's brother, told me that her father asked Mary Alice to get close to you. He didn't say anything more, but I know her father has got a reason for wanting his daughter to play up to you. I wouldn't say anything if I didn't think it was a serious affair."

"Thanks again, James. It's good to know these things."

Chapter 12

Expostulation and Reply

A WEEK ELAPSED and the order of the day had changed somewhat to include Jesse escorting Mary Alice to the post office each morning, early before the regular activities began in earnest. The two individuals had enjoyed some meaningful conversations during the time spent together and were getting more familiar with each other; that is, more relaxed and confident in each other's presence, more willing to share personal feelings. During that time, Jesse had sensed a change of attitude in the girl. She seemed to be a good deal less volatile, less apt to speak the first thing that came into her mind, more willing to be observant but not critical. It had been a welcome sign, he felt, for he had enjoyed her company along with the opportunity to get to know more about her family.

Not everyone shared the same opinion. Jesse's siblings especially were resentful of the time spent with the young lady. It meant less time for each of them to count on having Big Brother around to offer advice, to expound on the mysteries of life as they viewed them, and to afford them moral support in their individual challenges, such as they were, in which he had always been able to see "light at the end of the tunnel," so profound were his comments they were learning to accept.

Anne was also concerned for her son, recognizing that he had made a huge concession in his life, allowing for time spent with the girl, and speculating about his motivation in doing so. After all, he had become so patterned, so conditioned to utilize his time and energy in studying followed by working with Isaac and time spent alone pondering, she had come to expect that to continue until such time as he eventually left home. That personal schedule and use of time had become, to her anyway, something divinely established, something he had received from a higher source, which could not be repealed until now, that is.

Anne, Like Isaac and the children who had come to know something of Mary Alice—particularly James—was reserved in her thinking about the girl. She had heard things that were terribly unflattering about her relations with other boys and even men as well. She was colored as a flirt, even more so as a tramp, someone who had no use for morals or even decency. She came from a wealthy family but was critical of her parents and younger brother. She was spoiled, thinking only of herself, and not inclined to offer help to others including family. In short, she wasn't the kind of individual with whom her son should be associating normally. But there was more to Jesse than what could be observed on the surface, she knew, and it was her firm conviction that as he was spending time with Mary Alice, it was for a good reason and not something that was demeaning at all. She knew her son too well to think anything else, or was there…was there a man alive who couldn't be swayed by the antics of a beautiful girl?

Isaac had reservations about the girl that he had been reluctant to talk about. He needed Jesse's help more and more with his construction business, lately booming beyond his control. He had made commitments that needed to be kept and was working longer hours in an attempt to stay on schedule. Jesse, however, was spending less and less time with him, pursuing his own interests. Recently, the four days the boy had spent by himself had almost wrecked his plans completely. He was using every single daylight hour to catch up, and the threats made by Jerrod Houston had added a good deal more fuel to the fire overall. He didn't want to worry Anne, but the situation was getting more desperate with each new day. And today, the boy was gone again. Isaac had counted heavily on him to help in building and setting the ceiling trusses for the new home. His absence had made for an extremely difficult day at the site.

Additionally, he wasn't totally sure that Jesse wasn't chasing rainbows somewhere with Mary Alice Houston, who was a girl with a flair for the outrageous, using her beauty and body to lure others to commit sin. He thought the girl probably deserved what she received in the alleyway three weeks ago and then checked himself on the thought, realizing that he had no real proof of what had precipitated the assault. He did know something of the violent nature of the girl's father, though, and was trying hard not to condemn his daughter as well as a person without normal, healthy, natural constraints.

The family was together later, except for Jesse. The evening meal was completed, and dishes had been washed, dried, and put away, the kitchen cleaned thoroughly. The younger children had gathered in the living room for what was normally referred to as "family time," time when activities of the day were discussed and special needs addressed.

"Where's Jesse?" the youngest girl, Jana, wanted to know.

"Ask Mary Alice," James snidely remarked, "she can tell you."

"That's enough!" Anne intervened. "It doesn't help when you talk that way about things of which you have no knowledge."

"I know" was all he could say and then shut up, sliding further into his seat on the recently recovered chaise lounge.

"You may think you know," she corrected him, "but what you said was without basis and didn't help at all. Jesse told me that he would be late for dinner and would come home as soon as he could."

"What is he doing?" Jeri asked, looking at James.

"He's not with Mary Alice if that's what you think," Anne replied.

"Where is he then?" James shot back.

She looked at Isaac and then at the others in turn. "He's doing some pondering by himself. He doesn't really like for us to know when he's by himself because he doesn't want us to worry. He's okay, though. I think he's trying to sort out some things that need attention right now, that's all."

"About Mary Alice?" Jeri inserted, unable to control herself.

"I don't know," her mother said, lowering her voice to a near whisper. "All I know is that he said he would be doing some pondering and not to worry, that he would be home this evening probably."

"I hope he's planning on helping me at the site in the morning," Isaac inserted.

"I believe he is. Maybe James could help you too."

Isaac hesitated. "It's hard work and technical, too, building ceiling trusses and setting them in place. Jesse knows what to do."

"I can learn," James remarked coolly, "if I ever get a chance."

"That's good," his father answered. "I'll be able to use you in the future. For now, I would like to use Jesse while he's available."

"And not with Mary Alice," James couldn't help himself.

Anne stared at James and then at the others. "I would like to explain something to each of you," she began. "Jesse helped that girl when she was badly in need of help. He didn't stop and ask himself, 'Does she deserve to be helped?' He reacted that way because it was the right thing to do. Moreover, the girl still needs some help. Jesse says that her coordination has been affected because of the blows she took on her head. She gets dizzy and loses her balance. Jesse is helping her by stabilizing her as she walks. She can't do much of anything else right now. I know that some of you think that Jesse is being foolish, that he has no business helping the girl, and maybe you think that he wants to be a little more than a friend to her, I don't know. But I, for one, as his mother, know that Jesse has nothing but genuine concern for her. He truly wants to help her overcome the problems that she is facing right now as a result of her trauma, nothing else. Your brother is what is called 'a Good Samaritan.' He wants to help others, and that is why he is spending time with Mary Alice. And it's the only reason. Okay?"

"Okay, Mom," the others recited almost in unison.

"One other thing I might add," she uttered, studying their faces, "Jesse would be looking for opportunities to help each of you if he were here tonight. You know that to be true. That is his way, and he's not going to change. He loves people. He loves each of you, and that's not going to change either, not ever. When he helps Isaac, he never asks for payment. He works without pay because that's his way of saying, 'I love you and want to serve you.' That's Jesse, and before you start criticizing him for going with a young lady that has a shady past, stop and ask yourself, 'Is that the Jesse I know, the person who has never uttered an unkind word against anyone?' And if your answer is yes, then give him the benefit of the doubt, will you? I promise you that your confidence in Jesse will be rewarded on an eternal scale that can't be measured, not by man anyway." Her face was covered in tears. She had spoken with a mother's love and respect for her son.

Was she completely accurate? As a youth, still learning how to control his emotions, would he be able to resist feeling overpowering love and even lust for someone who seemingly had been blessed with more natural beauty than anyone else she had ever seen? It would be quite a test. Maybe, just maybe, this was to be one of his greatest tests of all...

As she pondered, the Spirit whispered to her, providing assurance that all was well. No words were spoken, just a feeling of comfort and peace. Be still, my soul, be still...

Chapter 13

The Relationship Deepens

JESSE WAS BACK with the family later that same evening, rather somber but full of expectation for the days to come.

"Dad," he called out after things had quieted down, "I can spend the week with you starting tomorrow. We should be able to get that house completely framed, together with the roof trusses set in place. You can count on me."

"That would be wonderful, son. I really need the help."

"Maybe James can be there some of the time as well so that he can start learning the trade."

"Yes," he replied after noting the look between Jesse and James. "He needs to begin learning all there is to know about carpentry. Not this week but soon," he added.

The next morning, Jesse met Mary Alice at the corner by her home and greeted her with a smile. It was eight o'clock sharp, their agreed-upon meeting time. Mary Alice returned the smile, thrilled to see he hadn't forgotten. He was dressed in his working clothes, overalls, with clips for carrying tools and equipment.

"You look like you're ready for the big job," she offered, returning his smile.

"I am. Isaac and I have a great deal of work to do."

She saw an opening and, as they began to walk, asked, "Why do you call your father by his first name? Shouldn't you just call him *Dad* or something more familiar, like pops?"

He laughed. "Dad is fine, and I use that some of the time. Pops doesn't work. He wouldn't answer if I called him that. He would probably chuck his hammer at me."

He had effectively dodged the question and so she tried to think of another way to force the issue since her father had scolded her for not getting any results so far.

"I hope you don't think that I ask too many questions. I'm anxious to learn more about you."

"I don't mind," he replied. "Some folks are an open book. All you have to do is listen. I'm not that way." And he grinned, adding, "How's that equilibrium thing doing?"

"Well, it's still there unfortunately, especially when I'm on my feet too long or strain to lift a heavy object, things like that. My mom thinks that I'm feeling the effects of a concussion. She's probably right. I get sleepy a lot of the time when before, I never felt fatigued. Also, I have passed out a few times, not for long periods of time but just brief intervals. I haven't said anything about that so please don't mention it."

"All right, but it sounds like you need to see a doctor. These symptoms are serious, Mary."

"I've tried to talk to my dad, but he just laughs and says you'll be fine and not to worry about it."

He caught hold of her hand and stopped her so that the two of them were face-to-face. "It has been long enough now that you shouldn't be experiencing any of these symptoms following that attack near the alley. Did any of those girls hit you with anything other than their fists?"

She thought back, closing her eyes. "Well, I think one of them might have had a blunt instrument, as I recall, or else it could have been a small blackjack. It knocked me out briefly. I remember that."

"Where did she hit you?"

"Just above the hairline, in front." She pushed her hair back so that he could see the welt. It was easily visible and appeared to be festering, red and purple around the base, and milky white on top, with what looked like a topknot.

He was alarmed. "I think you've got a problem, Mary. This thing needs to be treated. That blackjack, or sap, whatever it was, might have been treated with some kind of harsh chemical. At any rate, it shouldn't be bothering you now. You need to see a doctor quickly."

"All right," she relented and turned away.

"What's the matter? Did I say something wrong?"

She stopped. A tear had formed in her right eye. "It's nothing, really. It's just that you seem a good deal more concerned about the situation than either of my parents. They just laugh it off, as if it's nothing. My dad said, 'That's what you get for playing around. Maybe now you'll mind your own business.'"

He wanted to ask her what it meant to be *playing around* but held back. "Do something for me, Mary."

"What?"

"See a doctor."

She relaxed and sought both of his hands. "I will, Jesse."

They were at the post office, and after she came out, they walked back to their corner meeting station under the streetlight, now off. He was eager to get to the construction site but hesitated as she looked at him, constrained to hold on to his hand.

"Will you tell me of your father sometime?" she asked, a compassionate look on her face.

"Mary..." He fought himself for the right answer. "Who is it that wants to know? Is it Mary Alice, the girl I have come to know and care for, or is it her father?"

She confessed meekly, "It's my father, but..." She added, "I want to know all that I can about the man as well. I know this, he has a wonderful son..."

He grasped both hands. "I will tell you about my father, Mary, but there are other things that you must learn first about me before you can learn of my father. Are you willing to wait?"

She looked deeply into his unblinking eyes and replied, "Yes, I am willing to wait."

"Good. I promise, it will be worth the wait."

55

Chapter 14

Bailey Learns of Deep Secrets

JAMES WAS AT the mobile library site an afternoon later in the week, where he met Bailey Houston surprisingly, who was researching an article on nuclear fission for an environmental science class he was taking online. James was there to follow up on a reading assignment his mother had given him relating to shifting tides and how that would affect the earth's surface. Neither of the boys found library sources that were of value and were preparing to leave when the meeting occurred.

Bailey spoke first, "Say, James, it has been a while. What gives?"

"Ah, nothing much, you know, the same old stuff mostly."

Bailey herded him across the street where there was a snack shop, saying, "Let's get a milkshake, what do you say? I'm buying."

"All right, buddy. That sounds good."

The pair discussed a few topics of common interest, including the Internet and how they probably should have gone to the Internet first before checking the mobile library for current information.

"I knew better," Bailey said, adding, "Libraries aren't nearly so up-to-date anymore."

"No," James commented, "but as for the Internet, you do have to be careful about their source material. Sometimes it's not so accurate, especially on current events."

"That could be said of libraries too," Bailey asserted.

"Yeah, I guess so." After swallowing a cup-sized swig of chocolate milkshake, he asked, "What gives between you and Jesse now? I haven't seen either of you around for a while, except that Jesse has been chasing my sister Mary Alice around like a hound dog on a fresh lion scent." He laughed heartily.

James acknowledged that he hadn't seen Jesse passionate about girls before and that it was completely new territory for him. "He's normally a very private person," he contributed.

"Tell him to watch out, will you? Mary Alice is a hot number all right, but she can also strike quicker than any rattlesnake you've ever seen. And when she does, there's no antivenom. You're a dead duck."

"I think he has been told that and by more than one as well. She has got quite a reputation."

"Well, I know she's my sister, but I'd have to say that she has earned it. It hasn't come as a one-time thing."

"Personally, I'm tired of warning him," James finished.

"All right, let him be another in a long list of victims then. Say, what gives between you and him? Normally you're quick to defend your bro. Have things changed?"

"No, not really. We've always had our differences, I guess you could call them, but lately, it just seems to have grown more pronounced."

"That's interesting. What seems to have changed?"

They had each finished their milkshakes by this time but neither had shown any indication to leave.

James considered his response carefully. "I don't know. He's the same as always, a lone wolf in the forest, someone who keeps to himself but manages to find time to help my dad."

"I see," he mused, "and what do you think he does in the forest alone, as you call it."

James was suddenly defensive. "I'm not sure, and I guess I should keep my mouth shut since I really don't know. I would just be guessing."

Bailey pressed the matter. "What's your best guess, buddy? After all, you know him better than anyone, except maybe for his mother. Would you like another milkshake?" he added.

"No, thanks, Bailey." He shrugged his shoulders. "I'd have to say that he's trying to communicate with his father, you know, the guy who seems to have the greatest influence on him so far in his life. He ponders, he prays, he plans, I'm sure, for the future."

"For the future?" What could he possibly be planning for other than the ordinary things, like college, a job, and family?"

"He's not that way, Bailey."

"What do you mean? What else is there to plan for?"

"Well, you would have to know my brother in order to answer that completely."

"That's why I'm asking you, buddy."

"Okay, I'll give you my feelings, but really, it's just a guess.

"I'm all ears. What's your best guess?"

"Will you keep it to yourself? I don't really want anyone else to know how I view my brother and his preoccupation with his so-called father."

"Yeah, you've got my word, buddy."

"Okay, well, I think his father wants to remain anonymous, whoever he is, because, well, maybe the man doesn't fit in this world."

"You think he's an alien?"

"Something like that, or it could be that the man is a genius, too smart for society as we know it."

"That's groovy, man, an alien on earth. Does he look something like us, do you think?"

"I believe so."

"Wait a moment!" he exploded. "Does that mean that your mother had sex with an alien?"

James forced a laugh. "I didn't say he was an alien. I just said maybe he doesn't fit in this world. If he's smarter than the rest of us, smarter than anyone else who ever lived, where is he going to fit in? I'm just speculating, Bailey, and remember, you said you would keep all of this under your hat."

"Sure, buddy. I gave my word, but how is it that this individual, who is such a genius, you theorize, can communicate with his son then?"

"They've got some of the same genes, don't they? You don't want to sell Jesse short. He's brilliant all right. It just doesn't show sometimes, like when he's messing around with Mary Alice."

"Yeah. Okay, tell me what he and his father talk about then when they're together."

"I'll give you my feelings, but you've got to remember that I'm talking about things I really don't know anything for certain. I say that because nobody really knows Jesse for sure, including my mother or father."

"What's your best guess? This is far-out, man."

"Yeah, it is. I'm guessing that the two of them are probably thinking about how they can revolutionize life on earth, how they can make life more nearly perfect for everyone. That is, everyone who wants to buy into their concept of perfection. I guess you could call it a new world order, maybe."

"A new world order? Something that would affect the entire world you're saying?"

"It sounds crazy, doesn't it?"

"It sounds far-out for sure, and who would rule over this world order, Jesse or his father?"

"I suppose it would be both but probably Jesse since he would be the one on the hot seat most identifiable."

"The king of the new world order! Boy, you've blown my mind away, buddy. Tell me, how do you visualize what this new world order would look like? How is it going to be different than belief systems as we know them today? I say belief systems because I assume the order will have something to do with how we interpret our relationship with God."

"I have no idea, Bailey. I can only guess that it would involve a concept of a Utopian society, something without death and degradation, perhaps those things that are evil or the consequences of evil. Your guess is as good as mine."

"Do you think there would be a timetable of sorts that they would follow to put such a plan into operation?"

"Logically, yes, perhaps when Jesse feels like he has learned all there is to know from his father, the ultimate genius."

"Then it could be a matter of days, weeks, months, or even years?"

"Yes, or even a number of years, perhaps even a lifetime. Please remember, though, Bailey, this is all simply speculation. I don't know anything for sure, and you've promised to keep it between the two of us."

"And I will do that, James." He laughed, a snort really. "Do you think Jesse is looking for a queen? Is he intent on marrying Mary Alice so that she can be his queen? That would certainly derail his plans, I'm afraid. It would take her no time at all to re-revolutionize his Utopian society and make it a thing of earth, a fallen society, similar to what happened in the Garden of Eden."

"I hope that's not what he has in mind, Bailey. I certainly think you're right. It would be the opportunity Mary Alice would need to destroy all notions of a perfect society."

They shared a good laugh together.

"What a scam!" Bailey smacked James on the shoulder, and they each shuddered at the thought: *Jesse and Mary Alice together in Utopia!*

Chapter 15

Mary Alice Faces Her Past

BAILEY COULDN'T WAIT to get home and tell his father what he had learned about Jesse and his father. He was so fired up that he forgot that his own father was to be gone for another day, an emergency conference with his partner, Ted Barrett, which took precedence over everything else, according to what his mother had said. He took advantage of the extra time by cornering his sister, Mary Alice, and asking her some questions about Jesse and the Christian family, trying to learn a little more about them before going public with his father.

That notion availed him little at all. His sister contributed nothing of a negative vein.

"He's a good person, Bailey, and I do mean good. He looks for opportunities to help others. He does so with a caring attitude, not to be recognized and not to be rewarded. He is simply genuinely good. I've never met anyone quite like him before. He has had a strong effect on me, believe it or not."

"Oh, come on, Mary. We both know your gold rush disposition. You look for the mother lode, and if you can't find it right away, you strike off in another direction, always on the hunt, and usually successful. Am I right?"

"You're crude, Bailey, but I like your metaphor. I'd have to say that there is a lot of truth to the gold rush thing. But believe it or not, I've changed, and I have Jesse to thank for that."

"What do you mean? How could Jesse possibly have anything to do with making Mary Alice Houston something other than what her superb looks and instincts have made of her? You're a spider's web, a tantalizing queen of voodoo and seduction, a—"

"That's enough, Bailey. I don't want to hear anymore." She turned away, wiping at her nose. "I'm not that person. I never was, at least I never intended to be."

He was sober for a change. "What do you mean?"

She turned back, almost in tears. "I became that way because I had no choice."

"I don't understand. We all have a choice, don't we?"

"Sure, we have a choice but most of us are guided by our parents, aren't we, in the choices that we make?"

"Okay. I accept that."

She studied the boy, wondering how much to say. "From the time that I was very young, I was presented by Mom and Dad as a little princess fit for a prince. I was placed in situations where I was with the opposite sex a lot and was told and instructed how to use my charms, my physical presence, to lure others to do what I wanted with them in order to take advantage of all that they could give to me."

He was scratching his head, wondering where she was going.

"And it worked, it worked very well, except for one thing."

"What was that?"

"It backfired. It backfired because I found out that the best way to get others to do what I wanted was to give of myself sexually or at least the promise of sex. Do you understand now?"

"I think so. You became a hussy, hustling others for sexual favors."

She dropped her head and groaned. "Yes. I became something vile, something foreign to what I should have been, if I had received the proper learning and instruction on how little girls are supposed to be virtuous and cherish their moral nature, holding such things sacred for the time when they are married to the right person. I never got anything like that, Bailey, ever!"

"Wow! I never thought I'd hear anything like that from you, Mary Alice. This has got to be straight out of Sunday school. And you're saying that Jesse has awakened that sense of moral virtue to you now?"

She nodded. "He has. He likes me—I would even say that he loves me in a highly moral way—and yet he doesn't make any kind of advance that hints of something improper. He shows me love and respect, and he does so without the expectation that most boys have, of sexual fulfillment. He is simply a good person who wants to do good for the sake of goodness."

"Maybe he's not wired correctly," Bailey offered. "Maybe he likes men—"

"Bailey, you have no idea what you're saying. He is genuine. He likes everyone he meets. That's the way he is, a highly gifted individual who has enough love for everyone that he meets. That's Jesse. If anything, he's more than normal, he's ultranormal to a fault, almost. I think he would give away anything he had for a stranger if he thought it would benefit that person. He loves me because he wants to help me overcome my base nature, my amoral turpitude that has been sculpted so carefully."

"Speak English, Mary."

"It means moral baseness, according to acceptable standards, vile and wicked."

"All right. He's a good person. I'll give you that much. But, Mary, remember your upbringing. You're the Vamp of Seville. You're the Queen of Mean, Cruella Deville herself, the vampire that sucks the blood out of its victims…"

"That's enough, Bailey." She turned away, hiding her face. "I'm not that person anymore. I'm Jesse's friend."

Chapter 16

A Decision to Be Made

WHEN JERROD HOUSTON met with Ted Barrett, as instructed, an emergency face-to-face visitation without bankers, without accountants, without an agenda, he knew things were at a critical juncture. He was right. Ted Barrett was in no mood to be trifled with. He had endured several weeks without any monetary compensation to pay for the loans that had been secured to make the move to the suburbs that promised a future of financial freedom against a slow start, as foreseen. That move was one which he had been greatly opposed initially but had gone along with his partner against his wishes for the sake of goodwill, in the successes they had shared in joint business ventures to date. Now all of that was out the window in a flash if the company couldn't begin to show a profit for the controversial move that had crippled them so badly.

"Give me the lowdown," Barrett said when they were finally alone, "and make it accurate. Don't feed me any blue sky or otherwise."

"Well…"

"No ifs and ands, I said," Barrett coached him gruffly.

Houston took a deep breath. "Nothing has changed so far," he began. "We don't have any projects going at present. We're still at loggerheads with the man who calls himself Isaac Christian, the custom builder. He has a virtual stranglehold on all construction projects so far. I've tried to talk business with him, but he has rejected my offers flatly. He's old school and wants nothing to do with modern building practices. He's too ethical for his own good, but people love him. They're willing to wait for his availability because they trust him and because he does good work, though he's slow."

"In the meantime, we're losing $10,000 a day," Barrett groused. "Soon, it's going to be our heads on the chopping block. What do you propose to do about it, Jerrod?"

He rubbed the back of his neck, trying to ease the strain he was feeling.

"Give it to me, Jerrod, and make it good. What's to be done?"

He stared, blinked, and blinked again. "We're going to have to remove the opposition," he said finally.

"I agree, and it needs to be done quickly."

"I understand but, Ted," he added, "it's going to be expensive to get the right person for the job, a professional who won't leave a trace of suspicion that leads to either of us. You know who I'm talking about?"

The man growled at him, a first in their long relationship, "Of course I know! Then do the job yourself, or are you too squeaky clean for a job like that?"

"I can do it if I have to, I guess. I don't like it."

"Someone has got to do the dirty work, and you're the man that got us into this mess. Remember, though, it's got to be done quickly, whoever you get, or else both of us will be out on the street. And, Jerrod," he continued as the man began to stand, "we didn't have this conversation."

Jerrod Houston nodded, stone-faced. Perhaps it was time to call his good friend, Sydney Ventura. He hated to have to involve the man, but he couldn't think of anything else that could be done. Sydney could do the job all right, no questions asked. And yes, he was expensive.

Chapter 17

Bailey Strikes Out

THAT NIGHT, BAILEY followed his dad around after dinner and nagged at him until the man finally agreed to hear what he had to say about Jesse Christian and the Christian family. Bailey had never seen him so distracted. He seemed to be out in space, somewhere a million miles from nowhere.

Bailey started and told him everything he had learned: "The boy, Jesse, is planning a revolution. It's going to be something similar to a complete takeover of government and civic affairs with himself at the head, a king, over all. It will be a Utopian society I'm told, the perfect world with Jesse as the man in charge. And he wants Mary Alice to be his queen and is grooming her for that position. He has already brainwashed her into thinking that he is perfect, an idol to be adored, and is willing to go the distance with him no questions asked. He will establish the belief system based on what he has learned from his father, who is an alien, far-out in the cosmos, somewhere. The man is a genius with an IQ that is unfathomable by earthly standards. The boy, Jesse, has some of the same intellectual prowess being half alien and half mortal and is continuing to learn. When he has learned all, he will begin the revolution. He didn't say so, but I got the idea that anyone who doesn't jump on board will be exterminated. You know what I mean, Dad?"

"What, exterminated? Sure, son, I know. Is that all?"

"Yes, Dad, I guess that's all. What do you want me to do now, Dad?"

"Nothing, son. Thanks for the information."

"Sure, Dad."

A Life Hanging in the Balance

ISAAC HAD BEEN going to work each morning at daybreak, attempting to get as much work done as was possible before the daylight hours expired. He would usually work a full hour or hour and a half before Jesse arrived. Then with the two of them working together, they could make good progress throughout the day.

On this particular morning, he was checking the roof trusses, making sure the braces were intact before beginning the subroofing. There had been a terrible windstorm the previous evening near dark that had rattled the homes in the neighborhood badly, and he was sure the braces probably took the brunt of the near-gale force winds with the result being that the braces themselves—the support for where the rafters met—would likely have been compromised. He was standing on top of a twelve-foot ladder, examining the braces, when it happened.

He felt a sharp, sudden pain in the back of his neck that wrenched him badly, causing him to lose his balance and topple off the ladder. As he was falling, his right foot got caught in one of the rungs of the ladder and twisted his leg severely. He landed awkwardly on the cement floor of the construction site on his torso and lost consciousness immediately.

When Jesse appeared an hour or so later, he found the man lying in the same position, totally unresponsive. Checking frantically, he could find no evidence of breathing. He thought the man hadn't been in that state long but wasn't sure. His right leg was bent badly underneath him, and there was a good deal of blood along the chest area, showing vividly through his work clothes.

For some reason he couldn't explain, Jesse had been prompted to take his small cell phone with him that day before leaving the house. It was something that he spurned ordinarily because it drew his attention away from things that he felt were more important in his daily schedule and was a challenge, therefore, to his time allotment each given day.

Viewing Isaac's lifeless body, he grabbed for the phone and called 911. When he had given the emergency operator a brief description of Isaac's condition, or apparent condition, and answered the required quotient of question fired at him in efficient but rushed sequence hearing the response that was needed, he knelt and began to examine the man more carefully. There was a large bump on the back of his head. His chest had been penetrated with something sharp, perhaps one of his roofing tools which lay scattered near his body. His left arm appeared to be broken, along with the right leg. He was still unmoving without a sign of life, the symptoms of death written on his face like a worn map.

Jesse questioned himself critically: He was still young, not nearly ready for a miracle when needed or was he? Was his faith sufficient to be able to give life back to this man? Was he the person he needed to be to open the heavens and request that which an ordinary man could not do? He wasn't sure, but he knew that he needed to try.

He knelt over him and prayed, "Dear Father, bless this good man. He needs your help. Bless all who will attend him, that they will be able to assist him and restore life. Bless Anne, Father, that she will feel of thy strength and be able to lend whatever help is needed along with the family. Bless him with life, Father. Do this for the family, Father, I pray. Give life back to this good man…"

He heard the siren from the ambulance as it was heading to the construction site. It was near. He thought another siren was beginning also. Help was coming. He looked at Isaac who, amazingly, suddenly attempted to open his eyes.

When he did so, he recognized Jesse. "I—fell…" he uttered.

"I understand," Jesse assured him.

"Something…hit me…" he blurted, "my neck."

"It's okay," he assured the man. "I've got you. Help is on the way."

"Jes-se…" he forced out the words and then dropped into a chasm of darkness.

Once the two ambulance teams had arrived and determined the seriousness of the situation, they transported him to the hospital immediately.

Prior to that, as Jesse had listened to the conversation of the teams as they assessed damage to Joseph, he picked up the following: "The left arm has suffered a serious compound fracture. It will need surgery. The right leg is also broken, above the ankle, along the tibia. His chest has been punctured, probably a lung, as well his left. He has an obvious concussion, perhaps a fractured skull. He appears more dead than alive. He's hanging on by a thread. We're on the way to the hospital…"

Left alone, Jesse called Anne and informed her what had happened. "He is being taken to the hospital and is badly hurt, Mother, clinging to life desperately. He needs all our prayers."

Moments later, Jesse met his mother and the others at the hospital.

She was badly shaken but trying desperately to maintain her composure. "What happened, Jesse?" she screeched. "Isaac is always so careful not to have an accident since he works alone so much. He always uses a great deal of caution."

Jesse grabbed her firmly as he spoke, his two hands on her shoulders. "He must have been checking the braces on the roof trusses. There was so much wind last night that I'm sure he was worried about their stability. He fell from the roof and landed on the cement floor of the site. He would have fallen about twelve feet, Mother, probably landed awkwardly on his shoulders, chest, and head and neck areas. His head and upper body took a terrible beating."

Nearly an hour later, William Jerome, a trauma specialist and friend of the family, approached them from where he had been laboring with the trauma unit in the surgery center. He looked terribly haggard, beaten down, and exhausted.

"It's touch and go," he told Anne, wiping his face on a blood-smeared apron. "I wish I could say otherwise, but Isaac is badly injured. Most men his age would have died on impact when he fell. His neck and head took a terrible beating, along with his chest. He has a punctured lung, and the other one is most certainly bruised as well. He's catatonic, still unresponsive, barely breathing in shallow bursts. We're keeping him sedated. It's urgent since his breathing is so terribly strained and tortuous. There's a broken arm—a compound fracture—and a broken tibia that extends nearly to the knee. It's horrid in itself and may require surgery as well. He has broken ribs. I'm not sure how many at this point. His chest is such a mess.

"The lung will not heal, I'm afraid," he continued after wiping his moist face. "It is badly damaged. We've got to be careful that we don't lose the other one. The body is stressed, and the trauma may affect the other lung or even the heart. We're not sure. Besides those injuries, he's also dealing with a severe concussion…"

There was more, but she couldn't bear to hear the rest of the report.

Anne begged to see him. The doctor refused at first and then relented, even though he knew the man was sedated and comatose. She would not be denied. While she attempted to be with Isaac, Jesse went to the waiting room where James and the others were anxiously waiting for a report on their father's condition and filled them in briefly, withholding the worst from them, even though he knew it was bound to come out later.

James asked, "Is he going to be able to work again?"

Jesse spoke lowly so that the others couldn't hear. "Probably not, at least not for a long time. Right now honestly, it's a question of life or death."

"What about his construction business, Jesse? What does the family do while he can't work if he lives?"

Jesse had already thought about the question. The answer wouldn't be an easy one to accept. He wasn't sure how to present it to the others so that it would be mutually agreed upon. "We do the work for him," he finally spoke, "you and I, and the others do their part as well, as much as possible. It's going to have to become a family business, James, operating under Isaac's name and license, but you and I will do most of the work."

James looked at him in disbelief. "But, Jesse, I don't know anything about building trades. Dad never got around to training me, you know that."

"Well, your training is about to start."

The boy stared at the face of his brother. "And you're going to be my mentor, my schoolmaster?"

"I am."

"Are you that qualified, Jesse?"

"I guess we'll find out," he responded, "but I know one thing, I'm not going to let Dad's business die, not now, not while I'm here or can help fill in. I hope you feel the same way."

James hung to that utterance with his own promise: "Neither will I, Jesse. You can count on me so long as you're willing to lead the way."

"I'm willing, James."

"When do we start then?"

"What's wrong with right now?"

Jesse looked heavenward, still unsure whether his prayer had been answered or not. "I can at least do all I can to make sure the work goes on," he determined, "until we know for sure what will happen to Isaac."

On the way out of the hospital, he met one of the two ambulance personnel who had transported Isaac to the hospital. The man had stayed to see if he made it through the initial period at the hospital after he was admitted to ICU.

"I didn't have much hope for him!" he explained. "I've never seen anyone in such bad shape. We had to resuscitate him twice on the way. I was sure he was a goner."

"You did great!" Jesse lauded the man. "He's going to make it with God's help."

Chapter 19

A Discovery Heightens the Tension

ANNE SPENT THE night with her husband at the hospital in the ICU unit. In and out of consciousness, he had caused the nursing staff and emergency room doctor waves of concern and alarm, one harried moment to the next, wondering if the man would make it through the long night. When daylight finally came, the staff members were exhausted but hopeful. There remained a chance that he would be able to pull through the ordeal.

Anne was just as exhausted. Each moment alone with her husband in the triage tent had wracked her unmercifully. Each beat accelerated on the heart monitor was answered with an immediate pounding in her temples and chest. She thought each beat might be his last. She held his hand and prayed for relief. She was shooed away continually by the ICU staff, but she was soon at his side again, sure that it was her will, together with his, that would help him survive.

Finally, the doctor arrived and, after a cursory greeting, made an advanced check of vital signs.

That done, he read the nurse's report, checking on medication given and subsequent response, and then turned to Anne. "It's been rough, hasn't it?" And he smiled grimly.

"It has." She could hardly hold up her head, exhaustion overwhelming her.

"You need sleep, Anne." He ordered the nurse to prepare a strong drug to induce sleep.

"No, William," she answered quietly. "I'll rest when he's better, when I know that he's going to be okay."

"Anne, that could be days."

"I know," she breathed out. "I know."

"Okay," he said, relenting, "if he has the same kind of steel in his system as you do—and I'm sure he does—it won't take that long."

Before Louise Cooper, the ICU nurse, left for the day, she made it a point to talk to Dr. Jerome. "Have you seen the welt on the back of his neck?" she asked.

"Yes," he answered. "Why do you ask?"

She was reticent to speak further after noting the doctor's conciliatory tone. "Well, it looks like an open wound to me."

He smiled. "It is an open wound, like several others that he sustained when he fell."

"No," she replied. "This one is different, doctor."

"What do you mean, Miss Cooper?"

She demurred, not sure how to proceed. "I took a probe and probed underneath the surface a tiny bit," she admitted.

"Did you find anything?" he replied, now concerned.

"Yes and no," she responded. "At least I'm not sure what I found, but I thought I should mention it to you."

"Please do," he responded hastily.

"Doctor, there's something imbedded in the back of his neck. I couldn't tell what it was, and I didn't dare attempt to extract it, especially since it has penetrated the neck area an inch or so. But it appears to be something metal perhaps."

The doctor stared at the nurse before replying, "Let's have a look, shall we? I never dreamed that it was anything but a superficial wound when I first examined the area. I guess I was more preoccupied with his other more apparent injuries."

"Of course."

She handed him a probe, and he turned Joseph over so that he could observe the back of his neck.

When he inserted the probe, a few seconds elapsed before he spoke again. "You're right, Miss Cooper, there is something imbedded in the wound area, and it does appear to be metal." He withdrew the probe and blinked twice before announcing, "It appears to be engaged closely to the spinal cord, a dangerous spot indeed. I think it would be best to extract it in surgery. Please prepare the surgery center. It may be minor, but then again, it looks to be pressing on the spinal cord and capable of causing serious problems."

Nearly ninety minutes later, the doctor retreated from the surgery center to ICU waiting area, where Anne had been directed, and announced, "Anne, I just extracted a small projectile from the back of Joseph's neck. It appears that he has been shot."

"*What!*" She was dumbfounded.

"Yes, and logic now suggests that the shot was probably the reason why he fell off the ladder. If so, and I think it certainly fits, then someone attempted to murder your husband."

"*Murder?*"

"Yes, and now we've got an entirely different matter to deal with besides his injuries, which are of a most critical nature."

"What do you do now?" She was awash in uncertainty, the thought now pressing against her mind that someone had attempted to kill her husband.

"I've got to make certain that he is stable, Anne, before I do anything else, and then as quickly as I can, I've got to put a call into the county sheriff's office and notify them of the situation. That projectile, Anne, when I examined it carefully was forcefully resting against the spinal cord. It must have come within a few silly millimeters of breaking his neck. I don't have to tell you what would have happened if his neck had been broken." He closed his eyes, as if imagining the result. "Please, don't leave, Anne. I'm sure the sheriff will want to talk to you and possibly to Jesse as well, who has been working with Isaac. I'm sorry, but there's nothing else we can do. I will request that we put a guard close to where he will be stationed, whether in ICU or in a private room."

"Thank you. I will stay of course."

Chapter 20

The Investigation Begins

ANNE AND JESSE met with Tom Behrenger, the county sheriff, the following day, the first time the three of them could come together before Jesse and his brother planned to head to the construction site. He—the sheriff—had been briefed completely by Dr. Jerome the day before and had done some research of his own as well. He took time to report his findings to the two of them as they met in his office as requested. Sheriff Behrenger, a stout individual in his late forties or early fifties, was at first sight a no-nonsense individual, abrupt, and forward but with a patronizing nature, saving him in head-to-head conversation.

"The projectile, Mrs. Christian, was very small, only .177, when fired. It came from a smooth-bore rifle, meaning without any rifling, probably a pellet gun."

"*You mean a B B gun?*" she asked, bewildered.

"No, a pellet gun is more powerful than a B B gun. It can certainly kill a human at close range, whereas a B B gun would most likely leave a welt but nothing else."

"So you think the gun was fired at close range then?" Jesse questioned.

"Possibly," he vacillated. "But I should add, the fact that the bullet, or projectile, didn't penetrate the spinal cord indicates that the shooter was probably at maximum range. I would guess beyond thirty-five or forty yards. If he had been closer, Isaac would most certainly be dead."

Jesse kept silent, deciding not to inform the man what he knew of Isaac's earlier state.

Anne, however, swooned noticeably, unable to control her emotions.

The sheriff, clothed in full standard uniform with his service revolver and ammunition belt, realized suddenly that he had been too realistic in talking about the victim as if he were dead. "I'm sorry, Mrs. Christian. I'm afraid I tend to forget how I'm dealing with folks who don't ordinarily talk about homicide and its equivalent on a regular basis."

"It's all right," she returned. "I need to prepare myself to see things through the eyes and insight of others, as well as my own."

"Well said," he commented.

Jesse asked, "Is there a possibility that he could have been shot by accident, by someone who was firing at a bird, say, and who hit a person, a result of firing indiscriminately?"

The sheriff considered the question and then responded, "I would say no and for these reasons: one children, or adults, whoever might be using a pellet gun, normally fire at stationary targets or else at small animals. They don't ordinarily fire the gun indiscriminately because they're firing a dangerous weapon, something intended to kill or destroy, possibly at a skunk or snake in the backyard. Secondly if they're target practicing, shooting at a target for a score, they are careful to shoot exactly where they can see the results and accumulate a good score. The target is the proof of their marksmanship. Do you see my point?"

When they nodded, he continued: "Your husband, Mrs. Christian, was in a very compromising position when he was shot. He was on a ladder, perched twelve feet in the air, and totally unable to defend himself. There could have been no possibility of recourse against the shooter, assuming that the shooter had missed and attempted to reload and shoot again. He was, as we say, a sitting duck."

"Why use a pellet gun," Jesse asked, "instead of something more powerful, more able to kill at a longer range, where he—the shooter—couldn't possibly be apprehended?"

"Ah," the sheriff countered, "but a pellet gun is most certainly a lethal weapon, especially in the hands of an expert marksman. It fires a projectile moving over five hundred feet per second and is accurate within a quarter of an inch, at a distance of thirty-five yards or so. It's also quiet and can't be heard, unless you're very close, a must for a killer, who sometimes are given to using silencers or a suppressor."

"Do you think this shooter was an expert marksman then?" Anne inserted.

"Yes, we most certainly do without question. He, or she, whoever it was, was firing for the small of the neck at what could be considered long range for a pellet gun with intent, we believe, to break the spinal cord. That is quite a feat, mind you, and would most assuredly require the services of an expert marksman." He continued, "This person, whoever it was, was likely using a weapon that was scope-sighted—a special sighting bonus—with perhaps a laser aperture or sight fixture. The weapon was not something that could be purchased over the counter. It was specially made for individuals who like to kill things without having to explain to others what they've done." He smirked. "That's where we come in as enforcers of the law."

"Are you saying," Jesse asked, incredulous, "that someone put out a contract on Isaac's life? That a professional killer shot that gun?"

He looked at each of them without flinching. "That's what I'm saying, folks. We've got a situation here, and we need to do our best to find the answer. It hints at syndicated action or, at the least, of a professional hit job. Now what I need from each of you before you leave is a list of individuals who may have wanted Isaac dead. I'm talking about individuals who may have threatened him in any manner at all but especially with force, mentioning a death threat, say, or something similar, where not only he but also his family would suffer greatly."

"I can give you the name of a person who fits that description," Jesse answered. "He threatened Isaac just last week after he had refused to work for the man or to work for his company and was told that he would live to regret his action in a very frank manner."

"Who is the man?"

"His name is Jerrod Houston, and he is one of the two corporate owners of Houston-Barrett Construction that have been attempting to take over all construction projects in our area. When Isaac refused to cooperate with him, he made those threats against him and against his family, I'm sad to say. I was there at the time and heard every word of what was said."

"Thank you," the sheriff responded. "That could make short work out of our investigation. I'll keep in touch. Meanwhile, a guard will be posted at the hospital to oversee what goes on there, and another guard will be posted out of sight but still close to your home to provide insurance that you won't be attacked further."

"Thanks," they each said in unison before Jesse asked one last question: "Sheriff, I'm trying to visualize how this attack occurred. Isaac was on the ladder, off the ground, twelve feet or so. A shooter on the ground wouldn't have been able to shoot accurately at his head or neck area. He or she might have been able to hit him in the body somewhere but not in the head or neck, shooting from a position underneath him, unless they were quite a distance away in which case they would have been able to see his entire body. How is it then with a gun such as you have described, limited in range, the shooter would have been able to shoot for the small part of the neck?"

The sheriff smiled politely. "You are very perceptive, my friend," he responded. "The answer is, of course, for the shooter to be above the target and with his weapon, an air gun, say, shooting at a distance of perhaps fifty-five to 105 feet. That is something which we're going to have to work out, and I've got folks out in that area right now who are trying to bring that problem to a resolution. Stay in touch, will you?"

"We most certainly will."

Chapter 21

Work Resumes at the Site

THE FOLLOWING DAY, Jesse and James began work early, and Jesse outlined what had been done so far at the construction site and what was most pressing and needed to be addressed as quickly as possible. He had talked with Mary Alice the day before, explaining in person how he wouldn't be able to take time off to escort her to the post office and back anymore and that he would explain the situation as soon as he could. She had been understanding, especially after he told her that Isaac had been shot and remained in critical condition. She had voiced her sincere regrets tearfully, he noted, and agreed to meet with him at his earliest convenience.

"The framing will have to wait for a time while we catch up on some other things," Jesse explained to his brother. "We've got to focus on the plumbing tree as well as on the electrical conduits and outlets." He produced a blueprint for both the plumbing tree and the wiring schematic. "Dad had started work on these things, laid the foundation for further work but nothing more. He was focusing on the framing in order to do all he could with my help while I was available. The rest he was planning to do on his own."

"Do you understand these blueprints?" James asked, incredulous. "It looks like Greek to me."

"I do. It's not bad when you've had the opportunity to work with someone who explains it in detail and you see it develop from the ground up, finally becoming a reality."

A plainclothes officer appeared as the two were talking and introduced himself. "I'm Vincent Abrams," he contributed, holding out his hand, "and I'll be stationed nearby. You probably won't see me, but I'll be keeping an eye on things here."

Vincent was middle-aged, taller than most, and sunbaked. He walked with a slight limp. His weapon wasn't noticeable, Jesse saw, but figured that the man did have it hidden somewhere.

"Good," Jesse said, taking his hand. "That's reassuring."

Under Jesse's strict supervision the two boys began working together. The work was slow at first as Jesse checked and double-checked the blueprints to make sure they were in sync with the approved specifications and determine what tools and equipment were needed for each job, making sure those things were accessible when needed. By noon, they had arranged both tools and equipment where needed and could proceed with the implementation of the job. Jesse found most of the materials that would be needed and noted those that were lacking. For those that were lacking, he made a list, intending to order those sometime during the day whenever he found the time.

They had stopped for a short lunch break when Jesse looked up and noted that his mother was approaching. She was carrying a lunch for each of them, a welcome sight, along with a few water bottles. She looked distraught with good reason, and James asked about his father, how he was doing.

"He's doing better," she answered, her face drawn and haggard. "Dr. Jerome is pleased, calls him his 'miracle man,' and indeed he is. He will be undergoing surgery this afternoon to have those broken bones in both his arm and in his leg set properly. His spine is sore, very sore, along with his chest because of the broken ribs, but he's anxious to get up and start moving around. He complains that the bed is killing him, but I think that must be something else, probably the broken bones and the injured lung. He doesn't talk much—it's too painful. Though he hasn't talked of knowledge of the shooting or the fall, he apparently does remember things that happened prior to the accident, and that's a good sign. It means that his mind is active. He does have some effects from the concussion, though, as well as the punctured lung. The doctor is now hopeful that the lung will heal itself with proper care. I hope he's right. I'm anxious to get back to the hospital," she added.

"He's as tough as they come," James quipped. "Did you tell him that Jesse and I are on the job and not to worry?"

"I certainly did, but you know your dad, he will worry anyway."

"Oh, yes."

"Jesse"—she turned to her oldest son—"the sheriff wants to meet with us again. He says he has some other things he wants to talk about."

"Okay. Can it be tonight? We're going to be here at the site all day as long as we can."

"I'll check, son. Hopefully, that will work for him as well."

They talked further as the boys ate and then Anne left.

That evening, shortly after dinner, Sheriff Behrenger knocked at the door, and James let him in and then excused himself as the sheriff and Jesse and Anne met together in the living room.

The sheriff, always pressed for time, began the conversation. "My deputy, Jake Forsyth, and I met with Jerrod Houston at his office today. He's a smooth operator, didn't seem flustered at all when we accused him of badgering Isaac with a death threat, and produced an airtight alibi."

"Oh, what did he say?" Jesse inquired.

"He said he was in his office all day, together with his secretary. He produced the names of four individuals he had met with throughout the day, saying they would vouch for him in that respect, together with his wife, who was in and out throughout the day as well."

"Does that excuse him from being a suspect in the shooting?" Anne asked.

"The actual shooting, yes, until we can verify the truth of his statement. It does open the door for other possibilities, however, such as, there might have been someone else involved under contract to do the shooting, which is something we talked about yesterday."

"I see." Anne was plainly not pleased with the way things were going.

"Did you say anything about that to him," Jesse asked, "the possibility that he had engaged a hit man to do the job?"

He shook his head. "No, I don't want him to think that we're following that lead right now. We need to do some more checking on our part first, screening folks near him in order to find out who might fit in that respect as a shooter. That remains a strong suspicion right now."

"Surely—"

"I did want to ask the two of you, though, if you could think of anyone else who might have a grudge against Isaac now that you've had time to think about it a little bit more?"

Each of them shook their heads negatively.

"He is very well liked," Anne contributed. "He is a man with a reputation for doing good work and doing it within the time frame that is expected or specified. He is honest to a fault and very dependable."

"Of course," the man replied and then asked about his condition at the hospital.

She took the time to respond, bringing him up-to-date on everything that had been done so far, finishing with, "We still don't know how he's going to be affected long term, but we hope that he will be able to recover well enough to continue working someday anyway."

"That is hopeful." He hesitated. "We've learned a few things since yesterday."

"Please continue," she responded.

He eyed both of them. "I'll ask you to keep this information to yourselves," he continued.

"Of course."

"We've discovered that the projectile that was recovered in his neck has more significance," he related.

"Oh."

"Yes, it is .17-caliber as we guessed, but it is also a special projectile. It is made in Sweden and sold as ammunition for an air gun manufactured there, a high-precision rifle that is made specifically for serious shooters, mostly competition shooters, professionals who pay thousands of dollars for the very best rifles and shooting accessories that money can buy. The bullet, or projectile, is sold as a hybrid slug and is inherently extremely accurate, especially when fired from an air gun that is fitted with a carbon fiber air tank that can be pressurized to as high as 450 pounds per square inch, allowing for extra range and velocity."

"So you're saying that the shooter didn't necessarily have to be nearly as close as we discussed yesterday?"

"That's true. It's also true that the manufacturer of that product, FX Air Gun of Sweden, sells high-quality competition scopes that fit on those air guns, variable scopes adjustable in power that allow the shooter to have the target image magnified six times or any power beyond six up to eighteen." He whistled lightly. "That's a whole new ball game, folks!"

"Yes," Jesse concurred, "but at the same time, it also reduces your search area. How many folks are there who possess those ultra air guns? Not too many, I would guess."

"You're right, Jesse," he applauded, "but records kept of firearms sold go only so far. In some cases, the purchaser of a firearm, including an air gun, can be sold to another from the original owner to someone else without any paperwork whatsoever. It can be a problem. A problem occurs also when a firearm or weapon is stolen without record, of course. But you are correct in saying that the field has been narrowed considerably in this incidence when a match rifle and bullet has been used in a crime, in this case, a felony. Believe me, we are on this like flies on poop. Excuse me, Mrs. Christian, for being so coarse."

She covered her face with her hand, stifling her reaction.

"Did you find any evidence today of where the shooter might have set up for the initial shot?" Jesse asked.

"No, none, but then again, the field has been lengthened considerably now with this new information. We'll keep you posted."

"Thank you very much."

Chapter 22

Unhappiness Reigns Supreme

TED BARRETT AND Jerrod Houston met behind closed doors at a select location hardly known to anyone other than themselves. They were taking no chances, having disguised themselves fittingly, both person and clothes. Ted was upset, angry, and in no mood to be placated.

"Well, you screwed that one up, Houston. What do you propose to do about it?"

"Now, Ted, we're all right. I made sure of that. The man isn't dead, but he's in no condition to create any more problems in the construction industry."

"That's not what I heard."

"What do you mean?"

"I mean, he has two sons who are now doing the work for him. Do you hear me, they're moving ahead on schedule, and as reported to me, the work is as good as ever."

"Who told you that?"

"Never mind. I've got my sources. The thing is, everything you've done so far has just made things worse for Houston-Barrett Construction. I don't like it. I want out, do you hear me? I want out, and I want top dollar from you before this company started its downslide. You figure it out. I calculate that you owe me ten mil."

"*Ten million!* That's highway robbery!"

"You pay it, Houston, or else I'll go to feds and tell them what I know."

"Ted, you do that and both of us will spend the rest of our lives in prison. Listen, this thing isn't over. I guarantee you that things will be all right, but you've got to stick with me in this thing."

"I'm listening, but it better be good with no more screwups."

"Okay, now sit down and relax. Anyone would think your pants were on fire."

"My pants are on fire, Houston. What are you going to do about it?"

"Well, for starters, nothing I've done so far can be traced to either of us."

"You're absolutely sure about that?"

"Yes, I made sure of that. Second I've got enough dirt on Isaac Christian's family to put their construction firm out of business for good."

"What kind of dirt, and where did it come from? What's your source?"

"First the dirt: The boy, Jesse, is a half-breed but not a half-breed in any sense you've ever heard before. He's half human, half alien…"

"Oh, that's a good one, Houston. I've never heard that one before. Pardon me while I laugh, but it's hardly a joke you can scare a jury with."

"No, it's true. I tell you, he's part alien. His father came from another world."

"Yeah, and my mother is Wonder Woman, and my father is Superman. Now tell me another joke, will you?"

"I can't be straight with you, Ted, if you're not going to take me seriously. I'm telling you, the boy's father is from another world."

"Okay, who said that? Is that something the boy announced to the world. 'Hey, I'm Jesse, and I'm from Pluto.' Or was it Uranus? Next thing you're going to tell me is that he's the Almighty himself."

Houston backed up a half step and loosened the collar of his corduroy shirt as it had suddenly been pinching his neck furiously.

"The information comes from a reliable source, Ted. The boy's younger brother told it to my son, Bailey."

"Oh yeah? That makes it official, all right. Did you get it in writing too, signed by a notary?"

"I can't talk to you, Ted, when you're like this. Really, I need your help. Can you at least listen to me and try and understand?"

"I understand that you've got this company in a giant mess. I've got stockholders phoning me and screaming *Bloody Mary!* They're ready to sell and sell cheaply. We've got to do something reasonably resourceful and do it quickly, or else we're going to sink. And I mean the deep six, the bottom of the ocean, with no chance for survival."

"Okay, here's what I propose…"

"This better be good."

"I've got some more dirt on Christian's family, and I'll put it together and let you review it. We'll use what you think is believable to a jury and throw out the rest. In the meantime, I'll play up to the man, make him think that we're not his competitor but his ally, and then make an offer to buy him out. In his current condition, he'll probably jump at a chance to be bought out. That would be the answer to his problems."

"At least that makes sense, Houston. What kind of offer would you make? It better be pennies on the dollar."

"Oh, yeah, we can't afford anything more at this point."

"While we're talking money, how much is this latest screwup of yours going to cost us?"

Houston balked at the question and then did his best to cover up: "It was expensive, but I'll take the blame and pay the expense out of my own pocket. Will that satisfy you, Ted?"

"I suppose."

"I'm going to see us through this, Ted. You stick with me, all right?"

"All right, you get it going now, but you better sell this latest idea to Isaac Christian and sell it good. If you screw this up again, I'm going to see you fry in some wasteland in Alcatraz or worse."

"Ted, be patient. Everything's going to be all right. You need to trust me, okay?"

"All right, Houston, one more chance. That's all."

Chapter 23

Mary Alice Makes a Strong Move

JESSE WAS BOTH surprised and thrilled when he caught sight of Mary Alice entering the construction site just after twelve o'clock the next day. She had lunch for him and for James as well.

"I made a deal with your mom," she informed him. "I'm going to bring your lunch to you each day so that I can spend a few minutes with the two of you. I miss you, Jesse," she added. "I hope that Isaac is doing better now."

"He's showing a little improvement," he informed her, following the greeting and a polite little hug that didn't escape James' attention.

"Oh, good! I can't bear the thought that he's broken up so badly. You say he was shot and that he fell twelve feet after that onto a cement floor. How in the world did he survive?"

"He's very fortunate, Mary. The shot would kill most individuals, and then with the fall, it really is a miracle that he's still alive."

"Please, eat while you can." She opened the lunch sack and started pulling out the contents for both boys. "Your mom said you like sandwiches and fruit, so I made each of you a meat sandwich with an apple and a custard dessert."

"You made this yourself?"

"I did. That's part of the deal. I make a lunch and deliver it right at lunchtime. I hope you like it."

"It will be lovely, Mary. Thank you," contributed Jesse.

THE SONG OF JESSE

James was mute.

They started eating, and Mary continued to talk. "Is there anything else I can do to help you here at the site? Maybe I could bring tools when needed or just keep the site clean. Things like that."

"We appreciate the offer, Mary, but we're doing fine. If you can bring us a lunch now and then, it would be wonderful."

"Oh, I won't miss. I'll be here every day, I promise. I want to help as much as I can."

"Did you walk?" Jesse asked.

"Yes. I think it's all right now. Those girls haven't bothered me for a week or so. I guess they've given up."

"I wouldn't be so sure, Mary. They looked like they weren't going to stop when they attacked you before. It could have gotten ugly."

"I'll be all right," she assured him. "I'm more concerned about Mr. Christian right now."

James got up stiffly and grabbed his lunch and moved away, saying, "I need to check on the water hose, where I was spraying water on the fresh cement. I think I left the hose on last time I sprayed."

"Is he okay?" Mary asked when he moved out of sight.

"He's okay," he replied. "He's having a hard time accepting the fact that you and I are close, that's all."

"You mean he doesn't like me, or is he jealous that you're spending time with me?"

He finished the sandwich and started rubbing the apple on his pants, thinking about his reply. "Maybe a little of both, Mary. He doesn't know what to think. Our two families haven't been close. He has heard things that have colored his thinking somewhat. He's not sure what to believe. He'll be all right, just give him a little time to sort things out."

"He has heard things about me, you're trying to say."

"Well, yes, but also about your father. Your dad made quite a scene when he first came to Isaac and threatened him. I was there at the time."

"What did he do?"

"Oh, Mary, let's leave it alone for the present. I'm sorry I mentioned it."

She stared into the distance before asking, "What about me, Jesse? How does James feel about me really? Is it so bad that I shouldn't be coming around, bringing a lunch for the two of you?"

He put his arm around her and managed a smile. "I don't want you to worry about that, Mary. He will change his mind, I promise you. You haven't tried to dodge your past at all. You've been honest as honest can be, letting whoever was concerned know about things you've done in the past that may have offended them. You've been forthright in trying to change your image and be a special lady, the kind who wants to reach out and help others. I like you a lot." He added, "And James will too, I promise. Just give him a little more time."

"Thank you," she said and pushed her head into his chest, covering a low sob. She was hurt that James was so outwardly offensive but rebounded quickly. "Jesse, did my father shoot your dad? Is that what has happened?"

"I don't know, Mary. It's complicated, I know that much for sure. I hate to say anything when I don't know how this thing will play out."

"Tell me what you do know, Jesse?" she pleaded. "I need to know if my father is implicated."

He hesitated, unsure how to begin. "Why do you feel like you need to know, Mary? You can't change anything, not now."

"No, but I need to know how to react if my father comes to me and asks me to do something…" She couldn't finish.

"Has he talked to you, Mary?"

"Not since the shooting, but I think he will. I don't want to promise him anything if he's doing it for his good only and which will come down on you and your family. Do you know what I'm trying to say?"

"I do," he consented. He looked around to make sure James wasn't near enough to hear what he was about to say. "I believe your father is involved, Mary. He wasn't the triggerman, but my personal feeling is that he probably engineered the thing. But let me add,

Mary, we're going to be all right. Isaac is going to mend. It's going to take him a while, but he'll be back. Maybe not as good as new, but he'll be back. The family is going to be all right. Jesse and I are going to pick up the slack until Isaac is well enough to return. The sheriff is going to unravel this thing, and the guilty will be punished. I just hope that the result won't affect our relationship."

She didn't blink at all. "It's not going to affect the way I feel about you, Jesse, and I hope you won't forget me either."

"You be very careful when you bring lunch each day, Mary. I'm worried about you."

"You don't need to be, Jesse. Those girls are a bad memory, that's all. They've got other things on their minds now."

"I'll see you tomorrow then and thanks for lunch. It was swell. James will say the same thing, you'll see."

"Thanks, Jesse, and remember, you're supposed to tell me about yourself so that I can understand more completely about our relationship."

"I remember. The time will come. It won't be for a while, though, after all that has happened."

"I understand. I'll wait. And, Jesse, I've seen the doctor, and I'm being treated for concussion symptoms. He has given me a salve to cure the infection caused by the dirty club that was used to brain me with. Other than that, I'm good as new." She smiled and was gone, a fleeting ocean traveler swept away by the tide, leaving a dim imprint in the sand.

Chapter 24

Help Comes from a Strange Source

THREE AGONIZING WEEKS passed by, and slowly but surely, Isaac was beginning to get his strength back, along with his will to see that the family survived the crisis that had been dealt to them so suddenly. He was home and had decided to call a family council to review what had happened since the accident, applauding mainly the work of Jesse and James at the construction site with his wife's guidance, of course. He and Anne had decided that the younger children could also contribute in meaningful ways with odd jobs that were menial but necessary.

Jeri spoke first for the younger group. "Of course, we want to help, Father. We'll do anything to help. We want to help—all of us."

"That's good, Jeri," Anne spoke up, saving Isaac's voice, which still wasn't strong, neither was his stamina at such a level that he could remain upright for very long.

He was propped up on the couch in the living room as they spoke. She was doing what she could to take over in doing essential things for him, but it was also taking a toll on her, she realized, and was glad when Jesse suddenly stood and took control of the situation.

"I've made up an assignment sheet," he announced, "according to some suggestions made by both Dad and Mom. Let's go over the assignments and then get your feelings about the individual chores.

It won't be anything too hard," he promised. "We want everyone to contribute and also feel good about the opportunity to do so."

As they were talking about individual assignments for Jeri as well as John, Joseph, and Jana, the doorbell rang, interrupting the discussion. John went to the door and opened it.

As he did so, Jerrod Houston took a step inside and, taking off his grayish-white wide-brim hat, greeted the group: "I hope I'm not interrupting anything that's terribly important. Good evening to each of you." He waved his right arm toward the door and his wife, Sally, came into the home as well, carrying a hot apple pie, freshly made. "We brought you folks a pie. I hope it's a good time for dessert."

"It's always a good time for dessert with this crew," Anne responded guardedly. "Would you care to join us?"

"Thanks, I believe we will."

The couple came in and smiles and greetings were exchanged all around. Houston outdid himself in meeting with each of the children and parents individually and then impressed them all when he remembered their names and complimented each about either their looks or clothing, managing also to praise the home itself.

"This is a lovely home, folks. I admire what you've done to make it personal and attractive."

"You're very kind," Anne countered more brightly, "It's livable, even though it's not what you'd call a mansion."

"Oh, it's as sweet a home as I've ever seen," he gushed.

The pie was sliced into eight pieces and passed around, along with water.

"We've got some vanilla ice cream if anyone wants ice cream," Anne commented.

Accordingly, the ice cream was brought out and several of the younger set managed to cover their slices of pie with ice cream. The result was instantaneous.

"This is wonderful pie!" Joseph thrilled to announce, his mouth full of a sizable blend of both pie and ice cream.

After the dessert was shared and the couple had relaxed in the feeling of acceptance by the home crowd, Jerrod spoke to Isaac, who was still with the group but who hadn't been able to participate with talk or with the dessert. "How are you, sir? I hope you're going to be all right. It's amazing that you're able to be with the family already. I was told you'd be in rehab for at least six months."

He nodded but said nothing.

Anne spoke up, however, saying, "He should be in rehab. We're doing our best to stay out of his way. He's one of the more stubborn males you've ever met or hope to meet."

"I understand." Jerrod smiled. "I've met a few like him."

"You're one of them," his wife, Sally vouched.

That raised a slight protest from Houston, the equivalent of an "I guess so." He scanned the group before stating, "My company would like to help you folks now since you've run into a streak of bad luck."

"Oh," Anne replied, surprised.

"Yes, I've talked things over with my partner, Ted Barrett, and we've agreed to provide materials and workers to help you complete the work on the job site you're currently engaged on. What do you say?"

"*Materials and workers?*" Anne called out tentatively. "That's very generous of you and your company."

"Well, we want to show you folks that we think a lot of you. What do you say?"

Anne looked at Jesse and James in return and then directly at Isaac, who hadn't said anything yet but who had been listening keenly.

"What does Jesse think?" he spoke slowly, a hand to his throat.

Everyone turned to look at Jesse, whose eyes were still on his dad.

Isaac shook his head slowly side to side, hardly noticeable. Seeing that, Jesse responded, "We're doing all right, Mr. Houston. It's a swell offer, but we're on schedule and expect to be able to complete the job on time."

"Oh, that's a surprise!" he shot back. "I was sure that you'd need some help, and we're sure ready to lend you that support."

Jesse questioned his choice of words: "To *lend* us support? Does that mean that it's a loan, something that needs to be paid back?"

"Well, these are hard times for everyone, folks. We can provide whatever help you need if in good time, you're willing to show your appreciation by paying us back."

"Would that be at your cost for labor and materials, or would there be additional revenue, a slight profit, say?"

He grinned as the word "*profit*" was spoken. "Well, there would be a token increase if you put it that way, say a five percent increase."

"The answer is still the same," Jesse was quick to respond. "We're doing fine, Mr. Houston. Thanks anyway for the offer."

"Okay," he answered begrudgingly and then startled the group again, saying, "I wish you would reconsider. I've got another thing for you to consider before we leave, and please take this seriously. Houston-Barrett Construction wants you folks to have a payday now to lift you out of the cellar, so to speak, and give you a chance to rise to the top at this difficult time."

"Oh, and what would that offer entail?" Anne questioned.

"It's grandiose," he exulted, "something that can save you a lot of grief for a long period of time."

"That sounds good," she said. "Would you explain?"

"Certainly." He took in the room and group with an expansive gesture. "We want to buy you folks out, lock, stock, and barrel."

"Is that so?"

"Yes, let's face it, you folks have become dwarfed by the construction business. You're small time, a one-man show really, and the market is set to explode. It takes a big-time corporation like Houston-Barrett to be able to keep up with the demand now and forever as the industry becomes more and more competitive, especially with the regulations that FHA is placing on local contractors. It's almost impossible to keep up. It takes a company of lawyers just to be able to interpret the restrictions that are being placed on homebuilders now. It's shameful really."

"What's your offer?" Jessie inquired.

"You're a bit abrupt, Jessie, but that's all right. Let me explain in simple terms so that each of you can understand."

"Shoot," Jessie said and immediately wished he hadn't, remembering who he was talking to.

The man laughed, straitened his tie, and said, "We'll' give you $50,000 for the company and the home. Now if that sounds unreasonable to you, let me add, we'll give you 5 percent of profit sharing for the next five years. Now that may not sound like much to you at present, but, folks, believe me, it could amount to millions. It's enough to make each of you rich for the foreseeable future and then some. What do you say?"

"Profit sharing?" Jesse questioned. "How is the profit figure derived?"

"Oh, you're getting too technical for me, buddy. Let's let the lawyers figure that one out, but I assure you it will be enough to satisfy each of you for the rest of your lives. We're a twenty-million-dollar corporation, you understand. It's big business. We've got accountants that keep track of revenue sharing, such as I'm offering you folks."

"Can you give us an indication of what your profit sharing looked like in your annual report last year or in the past six months?" Jesse continued.

He did a quick double take before advising them, "It was plenty, significantly over a million dollars, I can tell you that without having the exact figure in mind for the past year."

"And you want the home too?"

"Yes, we would need the home for our construction foreman or other administrators."

Jesse looked at Anne and then at Isaac, who had buried his forehead in his hands.

Certain of his dad's feelings about the offer, Jesse replied, "And we would go looking for another home without enough capital to do anything other than make an honest down payment. This would be a very good deal for you, Mr. Houston. Thanks for thinking of us, but we're not interested in selling."

"Oh, I'm sorry, folks. We want to help you get through this crisis. It's our way of saying 'thank you' for all you've done in the community."

"The answer is still no, Mr. Houston. We're going to be all right, regardless of what happens in the future with or without your help."

"All right, folks, but I hope you have no regrets in a year from now when you have to declare bankruptcy and don't have a home to live in or food to put on the table. It will be too late then to ask for help from us."

"We'll get by, sir. Thanks for everything, especially the pie. It was delicious."

"There's more pie where that one came from. Remember that, folks."

"We will. Have a good night."

Chapter 25

Dead Men Don't Walk Away

SYDNEY VENTURA WAS a man without a country. He was a man without a name really, except for the one he had taken that allowed him to be drafted into the army, a name given him by the orphanage that raised him until he ran away and joined the military, claiming that he was draft age, a blatant lie but supported by a false birth certificate. He had learned early in life how to get around, how to be expedient when expedience was necessary, was demanded. He had exploited that in the army as well, advancing to the rank of master sergeant and concluding a second tour of duty with special forces.

It was there that he had gained proficiency as an elite marksman, even to the point of becoming a sniper, called upon as a hit man to target ranking officers and individuals of prestige in foreign governments, specifically the enemy.

Short and wiry, he was tougher than a convoy of battle-tested marines for he had done all that and thirsted for more, never quite satisfied. He had no knowledge of his parents, no high school diploma, short of a GED given as a prerequisite for entering the military, and no qualms whatsoever that he couldn't accomplish anything in life he set his mind to achieve. He was the master of his own destiny; more than that, he looked upon himself as a god, if you will, because he had the power of life and death over others, falling back on his assignment as a sniper, a licensed killer, a man who carried out the sentence of death for others, especially terrorists or villains as identified by those with money or power.

The army had taught him to be ruthless, to be unforgiving, to be an animal, really surviving on instincts honed by years of training, exceeding anything he had ever dreamed of in his premilitary years. To the point that he was now unfit for society, any form of society, even as a trainer of others in the military because he was too solitary, too unwilling to depend on anyone other than himself, too set on doing things without involving or answering to others.

So he had made the decision to expatriate himself from the military, from his country, and from close association with others. As a result, he now lived in a foreign country alone, without anyone or anything that hinted of family, except for a German shepherd dog that had accompanied him when he left the military, a five-year-old named Spike that had given him complete loyalty and love without asking for anything in return beyond companionship and an occasional back rub.

He got by in life by doing that for which he had been trained in the military, a hit man, and he was good, very good, as good as they come. He had hired an agent to take care of his official business, as determined by the agent, a man he had grown to respect, who was sworn to secrecy and would not betray him because he had once performed an act for the man that took care of an extremely delicate situation, something without a price that could never be paid in full. Because of that, the man would be indebted to him forever. It was a unique situation.

Because of his skill as a marksman and because of his disregard for the basic concept of morality, he had been called upon numerous times to be the triggerman in clandestine espionage and murder plots. The bonus in money had been good enough to set him up for life, but he continued anyway because he enjoyed the challenge each individual job presented. It was his chance to prove again and again that the low man on the totem pole could rise to the top of his chosen profession, taking down others more elect. And he continued to be paid handsomely for his prowess, so very handsomely.

His agent was the only person who knew how to contact him. All his business interests went through him, initial contact and payment, whatever was needed. His agent didn't know where he was, what country he was living in, whether he was alone or with others; he only knew how to contact him. The situation was working well, and he had protected his anonymity perfectly to date. He had a battery of homes that he frequented, moving around often so that no single person could get a fix on him.

Now a peculiar thing had happened: a man he had shot had suddenly reappeared in society. His agent had informed him of the aberration. A discussion had taken place between himself and his agent.

"The man is still alive."

"That's not possible. I confirmed his death immediately following the shooting. He was lifeless. There was no breath in his body, no heartbeat, no motion whatsoever. I've seen enough dead people to know the difference. The man was dead."

"You saw him personally? You didn't just assume that he was dead?"

"Listen, when I say I confirmed his death, I mean exactly what I said. I went to him. I stayed with him for ten minutes or more. He never took a breath. He was perfectly dead if there's such a thing."

"You went to him? Weren't you afraid you might be discovered?"

"No. I had done my homework. I patterned him, just like I do all my targets. I spend days patterning their behavior, their schedule, their idiosyncrasies. I knew more about the man than his wife probably. I knew it would be another forty-five minutes before anyone else found him. In that instance, his oldest son, Jesse, who was busy walking his girlfriend back to her home before he came to work."

"Jesse is not really his son but go ahead."

"I could argue the point, but no matter. I knew the two of them would begin work at from 8:00 a.m. to 8:15 a.m. That gave me ample time to say goodbye to my quarry."

"Goodbye?"

"Yes, I'm no robot. I get personal with those I target, as personal as I am with anybody, because I have no friends really. But when the end comes, I feel it's fitting that I spend a few minutes with them if possible and say a piece over them, sending them off to God."

"A piece?"

"Yes, a short prayer. I ask for their forgiveness for cutting short their lives. It's the least I can do, you know. Death is the end. It's final."

"Why is he alive then? Dead men don't get up and walk away."

"I repeat, that's not possible unless there was an act of God somehow."

"Okay, what do you intend to do about it?"

"Nothing."

"What do you mean? I tell you the man is still alive."

"And I tell you that I killed him and confirmed his death. If he's alive today, then it has got to be an act of God."

"Does that make a difference to you?"

"It certainly does. I'm not going to argue with God. If he wants the man to be alive, then that's fine with me. I'm not going to interfere. I did my part."

"I don't understand. Are you telling me that you believe in God after all you've been through in life?"

"Yes, I believe in God. He's the great arbiter. He decides who lives and who dies. If he wants this man to live, that's fine with me. I'm out of it for good."

"The man says you have botched the job. He says he won't pay you."

"That hurts a lot. When someone says I botched the job, they have no idea what it takes to do what I do and make sure that it never comes back to them or me."

"Such as?"

He found himself spitting into the receiver as he glared and spoke at the same time: "I spent a week patterning the man. After that, I spent three days in the top of an elm tree, teetering from a branch, waiting for the right moment—the perfect storm—when I could pull the trigger and end that man's life with no recourse afterward. You have no idea how difficult that is, to live in a tree like that for three days unless you happen to be a monkey, and I'm not. Armed with only an air gun, I had to have the perfect scenario, a shot at the spine in the back of his neck. A miss, and it would all be over. Then for any smart person who realized that his life was in danger, I would become the hunted instead of the hunter. I would have had to stay in that tree, motionless, while he planned his attack, his reprisal unless I jumped and ran, which I'm not programmed to do."

"So what do I tell this guy?"

"You can tell him anything you like. No, you tell him that God wants him dead. That is, unless he pays me a cool $100,000 and quick. That was my bargain price," he added.

"You're sure about the threat? He's an important big wig."

"No matter. God decides who lives and who dies. I provide the firepower."

"I'll tell him."

"Yeah and tell him it won't help to look over his shoulder. He won't see me coming."

Sydney Ventura was upset. No one had ever questioned either him or his air gun before. It was a personal insult. Suppose the man was alive, which he couldn't believe—unless the unnatural happened—he had done nothing that could be traced back to him. He was infallible in that respect. In over twenty-five years of service as a sniper, his name had never surfaced as a suspect in any shooting. He had been that flawless, and he intended to remain flawless as well. Question his integrity and suffer the consequences. God would end that person's life.

Chapter 26

Mary Alice in a Quandary

MARY ALICE DID not want to talk to her father, but he kept pressing her for information until she finally said, "Dad, I don't know anything that could possibly be of benefit to you or to your company. Maybe it's time you tell me what it is that you need, and I can do my best to help, if that's possible."

"I need you to tell me all you know about Jesse, the oldest boy. I know the two of you have spent time together. Surely, he has revealed some things to you that hint at who he is and something about his parentage. I'm trying to promote Christian and his construction business but can't do so without being able to answer a few questions about his family."

She was unsure of his motivation, remembering that he had been looking for ways to put the man and his company out of business just weeks before. "Why are you attempting to promote his business now, Dad? It wasn't that long ago that you wanted to dig up as much dirt as you possibly could in order to make it impossible for them to continue."

"I know," he admitted, "but things change. I'm sorry that Christian got shot, and I'm trying to keep the company going. It's a new me"—he smiled—"the nice guy on the block."

She smiled in return, a fake smile just like his. "Yeah, that doesn't exactly sound like you, Dad, the 'Master of Mayhem,' the 'Dark Knight.'"

"Ouch! That hurts, Mary."

"Well, it's true, isn't it? You have quite a reputation as a hard-nosed competitor, someone others don't want to do business with. At least that's what I've been led to believe, not from Mom but from others who are supposed to know of your business dealings."

"I'd like to know who those people are. It's simply not true. I've helped a number of individuals who were down and out. I'm just not good at shouting it out, that's all."

"I'm sorry if I've upset you. I know you're a swell father and have done well by your family. If I could help you, I would."

"But, Mary, you can."

They talked further, or rather, he talked, and she listened. He wanted to know every little detail about Jesse's life, anything that could be useful in promoting the family. And yet all she could tell him was that Jesse was a good person, a genuinely good person, with ethics and feelings for others that were beyond compare.

"He'll help anyone," she confessed, opening her heart, "even me. He saved me from getting badly beaten in that confrontation with those other girls when he didn't have to. I had bad-mouthed him several times unknowingly, thinking he was a pervert or a weirdo, someone to avoid at all costs. But, Dad, he's the best person I know honestly. Just being with him has changed me from a wannabe-witch to someone who can see good in others and who wants to be like him, to look for opportunities to help other people rather than put a hex on them. I no longer want to be a voodoo vampire or whatever bad people do, terribly bad people. That was where I was headed honestly."

"Okay, I can see that this is going nowhere fast. I'm getting a good picture of a person who has obviously found a way to manipulate your feelings in the extreme, as if you were under a spell of some kind, a trance, a bit of hypnotism. Has he done anything like that, Mary Alice?"

"No, not at all."

"Are you sure? Sometime when you were asleep maybe or too dazed to know differently?"

"No, Father, nothing like that."

"He did something to you. You're not the same Mary Alice I know—carefree, smug, and self-confident, callous of others and their feelings. I'm not being critical. I'm being realistic, objectively stating the obvious, as your father who knows you well."

She laughed. "Boy, you know how to lay it on the line, Dad. Was I really that bad? If so, I think I know the reason why those girls jumped me. I must have burned them badly."

"The old Mary Alice could do that in a flash. I've felt that a few times myself. But now really tell me something about Jesse or the family that no one else knows. Can you do that?"

She thought critically about each individual in the family as she knew them. "I don't know anything other than what others know, Dad. That's the truth. None of us know for sure yet about Jesse and his parentage, as you mentioned, but I do think that Jesse is close to telling me something about his father that will answer a lot of questions. He has promised me that he will share some personal information about himself. I think that time will come perhaps soon."

"Okay, I'll wait, but please don't forget. I need the information as quickly as possible.

"All right, Dad."

Later that afternoon, Mary Alice was invited to go with a few girlfriends and play cornhole in one of the girl's backyards. A cornhole set had been set up, and because she didn't know how to play the game, she had decided she would learn as this seemed like a good time. She had changed clothes, putting on some white shorts to go with a blue top, while the other girls waited, and together, they walked to the site.

Beverly, the host, quickly explained the rules: "The boards you see are twenty-seven feet apart. Teams are made up of two members. We divide up so that each team has a player on each side. Players are given eight bags and alternate tossing their bags for score. You can get one point if the bag lands on the opposite board, three points if the bag goes into the hole, and no score if you fail to hit the board. The winning team is the first to gain twenty-one points."

The girls divided up into teams, two on each side, one from each team, and began tossing the bags for practice. It was quickly apparent that Beverly wasn't a novice as every toss was good for a score, and two of her first six tosses went into the three-point scoring hole. They were having fun, noting who was able to toss for score and who was not, when three other girls suddenly came onto the scene unannounced. A glance at the girls told Mary Alice that she was probably in trouble. It was the same three girls who had ambushed her near the post office weeks ago.

They continued to practice their throws, but the fun had gone out of the occasion. The trio of uninvited girls began mouthing slurs at the girls in general but especially at Mary Alice.

Finally, Mary called a halt to the name-calling and said, "Just what is it you want from me anyway? I'm sorry if I've offended you. Will you take that as an apology? It won't happen again."

The girls looked at each other and began snickering to themselves.

Finally, the apparent ringleader, Corey, said, "We don't like you, Mary. We think you should leave town and forget to come back. If you don't, we'll make it so that you can't leave ever."

Mary was incensed but tried not to show her anger. "I've told you I'm sorry. I don't know what else to say, except that I'm willing to make it up to you if you'll give me a chance."

The girls looked at each other and smiled before Corey spoke again. "No chance, Mary. We like it this way."

"Have it your way then," she blurted, "but leave these girls out of it. They haven't done anything."

The trio joined heads quickly and talked among themselves.

Corey spoke for the others again: "We'll find a time to settle this, Mary. Not today but soon. If you're not out of town by then, it will be too bad for you."

And they turned and left.

Mary and the others tossed a few more bags and talked, but no one wanted to continue following the confrontation with the three rude girls.

Beverly said, "I know those girls. They're part of a gang. They make trouble for others and get away with it because their parents are wealthy and influential. It's a shame really."

One of the others, Sandy, said, "They mean business, Mary. You need to involve your parents as well as the police. Don't try and deal with them yourself."

She didn't know what to say.

Chapter 27

A Voice From Beyond

WHEN ISAAC WAS finally well enough to speak without the terrible pain he had been experiencing, he and Anne had a serious talk for the first time since the accident. They were in the living room of the home. The children were in bed or else away from home, expected back later.

He startled her by saying, "I had the strangest experience after I was shot and fell off the ladder at the construction site."

"You did? Can you talk about it?"

"Yes, I think I can finally put into perspective what actually happened."

"You mean you had some comprehension of what was taking place after you were shot and fell off the ladder?" She was having a hard time believing what she had just heard.

"Yes, I did afterward as I laid on the cement, and it's something I have a difficult time explaining and understanding because, Anne, I was dead."

"*You were dead, and yet you were aware of what was happening to you?*"

"That's what I'm saying. I was a dual person for a time after I fell, perhaps for twenty minutes or so. My body was on the cement lifeless, and yet another element of me—I guess it was my spirit element—was with me, close by my inert body, watching all that happened."

She was astounded beyond words with expectation of what he would say next. "What did happen during that time?"

He took time to recall all that he had seen: "A man, a small man dressed in camouflage clothing, his face covered with dark greasepaint under his eyes and over his eyebrows, came to me and checked to make sure that I was dead." He paused. "And then strangely enough, he began to pray over me."

"Pray over you?" She couldn't believe what she was hearing.

"Yes, incredibly he asked me to forgive him for killing me and then asked God to take my soul. It was kind of touching really. I almost think I could forgive him."

She was nonplussed. "Did he have his weapon with him, the rifle he shot you with?"

"No, there was no rifle, just the man dressed in camos with a front brim hat, a baseball hat pulled low over his face. After he prayed, he left."

"What happened then?"

"It was a while before Jesse came to the site. I was still dead I guess because my dual self was still with me, and after Jesse came, he prayed over me too. And, Anne, Jesse asked that my life be restored, and that's when my spirit entered my body again. It was amazing. My spirit element came back into my body as he prayed for me. I don't know anything about what happened after that. I was more dead than alive for a time, I think, but my will to live was stronger than my will to die, I know that. And it was all made possible by Jesse's prayer."

"Isaac, this is terribly important. Do you think you could describe what happened to you to Sheriff Behrenger?"

He considered the request. "Parts of it I could. I wouldn't want to tell him everything I've told you, but I could certainly tell him of the fellow who shot me. I doubt if he would believe me, though, he's a black-and-white type individual, I know from experience."

"Isaac, he might if you can describe this person who shot you. Do you think that you can describe him in more detail?"

He thought for a minute. "Well, I could try. He was small, as I say, and had dark features, but it was hard to tell with all the grease-paint he had splattered on his face. I would say that he was Anglo, probably in his late forties or early fifties. He appeared to me as possibly someone with a military background with military-type boots. His hat was brownish green with no markings. He talked kind of like an Easterner, a person from Jersey perhaps, with a Jersey-type accent, and he had a pistol holster on his hip with what looked like a Mauser or German Luger."

"Was the hat a baseball cap or a beret?"

"It was a cap, similar to what a military commander might wear."

"Isaac, this is terribly important. We've got to contact Sheriff Behrenger immediately and share this information with him."

"But, Anne, I don't think he will believe me. I'm not sure he believes in God.

"He will after you describe the person. And with that description and the part about being an army person, a leader even, he may even be able to identify the person. Then he'll have to believe you. Isaac, this could be the answer not only to who shot you but, also, who it was that was responsible for the shooting! I think it's a miracle. God wants to help Sheriff Behrenger solve this riddle, whether he believes in him or not."

"You may be right, Anne. We'll see what happens. He may just treat it as a dream or a hallucination, something that happens when a person is under extreme stress, when an individual's life is slipping away and he's more dead than alive."

"Well, I certainly believe you that it happened just as you said. I'm going to contact Sheriff Behrenger now and let him know that we need to talk."

"All right, Anne. I've been keeping this to myself, but I think you're right, it needs to be said. It could be the answer to what happened all right, strange as it may seem, an example of the dead speaking from the grave, almost made possible by Jesse..."

"Oh, how I love that boy and to think that he could do something like that, give you back your life. It's wonderful but also scary, a kind of premonition of what's to come in his life." She hustled away to contact Sheriff Behrenger, her mind still in a dither over what she'd just heard.

* * * * *

The next day, following the conversation between Isaac and Anne and Sheriff Behrenger, the sheriff had this comment: "I've never heard such a strange thing, Isaac, but I want to believe you. I know others have made claims similar to yours. I don't know if we could ever in a million years convince a jury of what you've just related, however, unless I can take this information that you've passed along and find this man you've done such a good job of describing. If he's still alive, we'll find him, and based on what you've been able to say, I think we can come up with enough evidence to convict him, working backward in this case. It's going to be quite a challenge because we have no hard evidence other than your statement, and one other thing…"

"What's that?" Isaac asked.

"We found a part of a footprint at the scene, one that was different than that of what you were wearing or even of Jesse and his footwear. It was a partial footprint of a boot. Now after what you've said, I would guess that it could be a military combat boot print. That's a good lead, and we'll check it out. Also, we've found the tree that the shooter used from which he fired the shot. We've got evidence of slight changes made to the tree to accommodate his stay there. It appears that he was in the upper portion of the tree for several days. We're attempting to match up scratch marks found on the limbs and trunk of the tree with the partial print found at the construction site. This could certainly be a breakthrough, too, especially with what you've told us today. It does appear that this man, whoever he was, was an individual with a military background and perhaps even as a sniper in Southeast Asia. We're going to go full speed ahead now and check these things out. Thanks for all you've said. I think we're on the right track."

"Let me know if I can help you further," Isaac commented, thrilled at what the sheriff had said.

"I will. This is an incredible breakthrough. Thanks ever so much! Our next step will be to dig up photos of military personnel that had experience as snipers in the Vietnam conflict. Once we have those photos, we'll have you come in and go over them. Hopefully, you'll be able to identify the shooter at that time. It will be difficult, I know, because of the greasepaint on his face. As a former deputy, you know what this procedure will involve?"

"Yes, certainly."

"One other thing," he warned, "don't forget that the shooter may still be looking for an opportunity to finish the job since it's apparent now that you survived. Surely his client, the person who hired him, will be putting pressure on him to do so. You've got to be extremely cautious. We've still got security staff out at your home and at the construction site, watching for suspicious activity, but we can't protect you 24-7. It's just not possible. You've got to be aware of that fact."

"Thank you, and yes, I'm aware of the danger. We're attempting to cope with it."

"Good. Keep it up. Now we've got to go to work and see what we can do with the information you've just given us."

Chapter 28

A New Ball Game

MARY ALICE HAD her mother take her to the construction site the next day with lunch for Jesse and for James with instructions to pick her up in thirty minutes, so she would be able to stay during the lunch break and talk with Jesse. The two boys had been working furiously in an attempt to finish up the building project and were drawing close. James was doing some prep work prior to beginning the painting of the outside of the home, and Jesse had been working on cabinets and other furnishings inside.

"What else have you got to do?" she asked Jesse as they sat together on the steps of the front porch recently completed.

"Oh, we've still got plenty to do, including the painting, inside and out, along with trim and specialty work. I've got cabinets to assemble and paint, and then we've got floor coverings to work on. Finally, we've got to form and pour the driveway and back porch areas and complete the garage inside. The buyer wants cabinets and shelves along the interior of the garage too. There's still three weeks of work left at least."

They talked idly for a few minutes and then she dared ask, "Has there been anything new happening regarding the shooting? Have the sheriff and his officers come up with anything new yet about who it was that did the shooting?"

"They're not saying much," he replied, "but there has been a new development."

"Oh, in what way?"

He paused, wondering how much to share. "Isaac has given them some information that might be useful," he stated matter-of-factly, remembering that the sheriff had given out the description of the shooter that he had given them and that it was to be released that evening to the national news agencies.

She peered keenly at him, expecting an explanation which didn't come. "What do you mean?" she prompted.

He argued with himself then said, "It appears that he saw the shooter and was able to give them a partial description of the man."

"*Really?*"

"Yes, and if the sheriff and his folks are able to find the fellow who fits the description that he gave them, it could lead them to the shooter anyway, who was probably a hired individual."

"Hired? Then you think that the person responsible for the shooting is another individual entirely?"

"That's the belief. The shooter was probably a professional killer or hit man."

"Wow! This sounds just like the movies: *Have Gun – Will Travel*, that sort of thing."

He laughed. "Yes, except that television series goes back a half a century or more. I've seen a few reruns, and it was good in its day. There was even a song that went with the title."

She was amused. "Can you sing it?"

"Mary, you'd die laughing if I tried to sing. I can't tell one note from another. It's that bad."

"You're too modest, you know. I bet you could sing with the best of them if you put your mind to it." She started to prepare to go and then remembered the confrontation with the three girls from yesterday and said, "I had another run-in with those girls who ambushed me just yesterday."

"Is that why you had your mother bring you today?"

"Yes, and she's going to pick me up in a few minutes as well."

"Did they threaten you again?"

"They did. I tried to make friends with them, but they'll have none of it. I'm afraid they're not going to be happy until they have their way with me, whatever that is."

"Mary, you be extra careful. Those girls can be mean."

"I'm afraid you're right. Believe me, I'm not going to take any chances. I'll come with Mom or else with Bailey. Maybe I'll get a dog too, a fierce mongrel that bites everybody but me." She laughed again. "You think that would work?"

"Maybe if he's fierce enough. Make sure you don't come by yourself, though, even with a dog. You're asking for trouble when you do."

"You're right. I promise I'll be careful."

Her mom had come as they were talking, and she excused herself.

Before going, she bent over and kissed him on the cheek, saying, "I wish we could spend more time together, Jesse. I miss you," and she smiled sweetly.

"Me too," he replied and brought his lips together, mimicking her kiss.

* * * * *

That night, after Mary's dad came home, he inquired of her, "Did you learn anything new about Jesse and his family?"

"Maybe," she responded.

"*Maybe what?*" He was instantly upset with her vague response, and it showed.

"Maybe I'll tell you and maybe I won't if you're going to be angry."

"I'm sorry, sweetie. I've had a hard day. Please, tell me."

"Okay, well, it's not really about the family, but it might be interesting anyway."

"Like what?" he coached her.

"Jesse told me that his dad was able to give the sheriff and his bunch a partial description of the man who shot him."

"*What!*"

"That's what he said, Dad."

The man was stunned into silence for a few seconds. "How was he able to give the police a description if he was unconscious after it happened, totally insensible with his eyes closed?"

"I have no idea, Dad. I only know what I told you, the police have a partial description of the man who did the shooting."

He was visibly upset, so much so that his agitation returned. "What kind of description did he give the officers, Mary? Did he say? Think hard. This is important."

"I don't know, Dad, only that the description might lead to the shooter and, in turn, to the person who was responsible for wanting Isaac dead. That's all that was said."

His hand went to his face in dismay, and he slowly turned and walked away, mumbling, "It's just not possible…"

Chapter 29

"Air Raid!" Take Warning!

SYDNEY VENTURA'S AGENT contacted him immediately with the news that a partial description had been released of the shooter in the Isaac Christian shooting followed by a plea to the public for information leading to the arrest of the suspect in question.

"What information did they give out," he questioned, "regarding the description? Was it accurate?"

The agent spoke lowly and succinctly as they conversed over the highly secure line. "It's vague but has some essential elements in it, like clothing, size and weight, and possible ethnicity. The person who gave out the description must have gotten a good look at you. It almost sounds like he was there, he or she, whoever it was. They mention the face was shrouded in greasepaint and said the person may have a military background."

"*Really!* I don't see how they could have picked up all that information. I was very careful not to be seen."

"Well, you were, that much is evident. It will take time now, but sooner or later, they will come up with a positive ID. You need to make sure you're not available for interrogation. Do you understand me?"

"Of course. They're not going to be able to trace me unless you've given out information that can point back to me."

"I've done no such thing. I know better than that."

The line went silent briefly before Ventura asked, "Has anything changed with the victim's condition?"

"Only that he's improving slowly and has begun to talk freely. Tell me, is it possible that he could be the person who gave out the description?"

The answer was emphatically given: "No, that's not humanly possible unless God taped the scene and played it back later for his benefit. The man wasn't in la-la land. He was in heaven, or hell, one or the other."

"It must have been heaven then. If he hadn't have had angels or cherubs or some kind of divine help, we wouldn't be having this conversation."

"I believe that. It makes me want to go back and make sure he doesn't say any more."

"Leave it alone, Syd. Things are bad enough as it is."

"I know. I'm gone. They'll never find me. One other thing, did they give any information about who gave them the description?"

"No, of course not. They're protecting the informant."

"Naturally. Just thought I'd try."

"You stay hidden, Syd."

"Gotcha."

Chapter 30

Isaac Retaliates

ISAAC SPENT THE next several days going through a collection of photographs assembled of individuals with a military background that also had some experience as a sniper or of specialized marksman duty. There were also several books of mug shots of former felons or convicts who had been involved in shootings, such as had mirrored his situation. Honestly, he was almost sorry that he had mentioned what happened when the lights went out at the construction site and he became a victim of the shooting, saved by help he couldn't explain to others, except to say that it did happen. Of that, he was certain for he was alive, given another chance at mortality, and knew because of that special dispensation, he had to make the best of things as they were, including staring at thousands of faces to determine which ones could or couldn't be the face of the shooter that had put out the light initially.

Finally, after the fourth day of scrutinizing photos, until he was so exhausted that he couldn't hardly tell one photograph from another without staring fixedly for what seemed like several agonizing seconds, he had come up with a total of nineteen photos that he handed over to Sheriff Behrenger, saying, "This is the best I can do. The shooter might be one of these men. It was extremely difficult because his face was so distorted by greasepaint. I focused on facial contour and tried to match up eyebrows and nasal features. I hope I've got the man in here somewhere."

"All right, Isaac," he replied, patting him on the back carefully because he was still extremely sore throughout his body, and his broken bones were screaming for relief. "We'll take it from here. We'll go through this list now and start culling for temporary status, finding out which of these are still active and in what manner, that is, what they're currently doing and whether that activity might coincide with what happened at the construction site on the day you were shot. Our men will check their location and triangulate it with yours when the shot was fired. We'll double-check alibis and determine which are valid or not. We'll be going over these fellows with a fine-tooth comb, determine their family status, or lack of, along with myriad other things. It's going to be a lengthy process, but by the time we're finished, we'll have the list narrowed down to a few possible suspects. We only hope the shooter will be one of them."

"I hope you're right. I've done the best I can."

"You've done wonderfully, especially since you should probably still be in the hospital…"

"Or dead," he added.

"Yes, that too. Now before you go, I'll say that we're still guessing that the shooter has a military background. We may be wrong on that suspicion. If so, then this will possibly be an exercise in futility, but I have a feeling that our shooter is one of these nineteen men and that you've laid the groundwork to lead us to him. I hope I'm right."

"So do I. I don't want to have to cull more photographs of a face that was mostly hidden from view anyway. It's a stab in the dark at best."

"You're right, but it's things like this that often make a difference in solving difficult cases like yours. You, my friend, have gone the extra mile. We'll take it from here. You've given us the ammunition we need to be able to go forward. Thanks again."

As he was leaving, Isaac remembered to ask, "Has there been any suspicious activity seen either at the construction site or at our home that we need to be aware of?"

"Nothing so far. Let's hope it stays that way."

Chapter 31

Jesse and James, Head-to-Head

JESSE AND JAMES had stopped work at the site, allowing a few minutes to rest and relax a bit; the work had been going at such an accelerated pace.

Jesse was pleased with the way the younger boy had warmed to the construction business and told him so, "You're certainly doing well with everything we've done so far, James. You appear to be a natural at this kind of work, with skills that will only get better with time. I know Dad will be pleased."

They were currently expecting a truckload of plywood to finish up the subflooring of the home.

"I enjoy the work," he offered. "It's difficult but rewarding, especially when you get to see the project take shape. Thanks for giving me the chance."

"It was necessary. I'm pleased with the way you've shouldered your part of the load. I couldn't have done it without you."

"You've been a good teacher," he imparted freely. "I had no idea you were so well informed in all aspects of building trades."

"That a credit to Dad. He's been patient with me."

"I wish he'd given me some of that patience as well. I've wanted to help."

"Well, it's your turn now. It won't be that long before I'll be gone anyway, and you'll have a much greater responsibility, you and the others as well."

James wasn't sure how to take that remark. "You'll be gone? Do you mean for good?"

"Possibly. Things are taking shape for me, James. I'm close to an understanding of what is expected and how I'm supposed to assert myself, in life I mean. It's going to be quite an adventure. I say adventure, but really, it's more than that. It will be a life's work, doing all I can to further God's work throughout the kingdom."

"The kingdom?"

"Yes, throughout the world, I mean."

"You're kidding me, aren't you?"

"No, James, I'm serious."

He stared blankly, not comprehending. "When you speak of life's work, what do you mean? You're not talking about building houses, are you?"

Jesse forced a laugh and then quickly became serious. "No, I'm talking about doing God's work here, among his children."

"What is it you're going to be doing, Jesse, that you call God's work?"

"There's a lot of things involved in that work, more than I could possibly explain in a day or so even, but, James, God's work revolves around teaching all individuals of every denomination and ethnicity how to worship God correctly. It is also a plan for the salvation of mankind. It is a way of life that opens the door so that each of us can return to God, our Father."

"Wow! That's quite a mouthful!"

"Yes, it certainly is."

"But, Jesse, doesn't the world as we know it already have the answers to what it takes to become like God as those things are recorded in Scripture?"

"Oh, yes, but there are also a great many different interpretations of those things. I want to clarify those different interpretations so that each person can have a clearer view of what is expected of him or her in order to return to live with God again."

He mused over what had been said. "How do you think people will receive your new teachings, your new interpretation of Scripture?"

"There will be some who will accept and some who won't. My job will be to present what God has given me to share and to allow folks to make up their minds, whether to accept it or not."

"Some who are deeply steeped in their religious views will likely become upset with what you have to say."

"Yes, there are those. That is to be expected."

"Some may even try to stop you, become a serious threat…"

"Yes, I suppose so. There is always danger in going against the established norm, especially in sharing religious viewpoints."

"Does that scare you? I would certainly be afraid of what might happen."

"Scare? I'm not sure that's the right word. I'm apprehensive, yes, and with that, there comes an element of fear. It's fear of the unknown, not sure if I can be equal to what it is I'm asked to do. I'm still learning after all. I'm not perfectly sure what trails to follow if you get my understanding. I'm afraid of failure. Let's put it that way."

James studied the face of the other carefully before asserting, "You're going to be just fine, Jesse. I know you well enough to say you'll do whatever it is that is required and probably a good deal more as well."

"Thank you for your trust."

"Are you ever going to marry, Jesse? Will you become a family man?"

It was time for Jesse to stop and consider the answer to the question. "I'm really not sure, James. I would have to say probably not. The way I see my mission, or calling, is that I will be on the move constantly, attempting to reach as many people as possible. In that event, I doubt if I will have time to marry and raise a family."

"What about Mary Alice? She will be disappointed. I saw her kiss you on the cheek. I know she loves you."

"And I love her but in a different way than you can conceive of right now."

"You should get married at some point in time, I think."

He considered the suggestion carefully. "Mary Alice is an affectionate person, someone who needs love but hasn't found it yet, at least not the kind of love that leads to success at home. She hasn't been shown much love by her parents unfortunately. They are career-type people and have put their careers before their family. It is failing and Mary Alice is searching for acceptance and for love. I feel like she will find it in time. It will probably not be found with me, however."

"That's a shame. I think the two of you would go together if it ever happened."

"I wouldn't discount the possibility completely. But we're both young, and it may take her more time to find the right person with which to share her love. It will likely happen for her at some point in time if she is truly searching and determines correctly what values to seek for in mortality."

"You sound so philosophical, Jesse. How did you get that way?"

He grinned then quoted Henry David Thoreau, the American naturalist, poet, and homespun philosopher, "I've always been regretting that I was not as wise as the day I was born."

"What is that supposed to mean?"

"It means different things to different people, but for me, it means that I came to earth with a firm understanding of what was to be expected of me and now, following birth, the plan has been muddied considerably. Each day it becomes a little less clear as mortality becomes more pronounced and encroaches on my spiritual nature. Does that make sense?"

"When you put it that way, yes, it makes sense. But, Jesse, I think you should seriously consider marrying Mary Alice in the future sometime. You two are meant for each other."

He shrugged it off, saying, "I feel deeply for Mary Alice, but I fear that her destiny in life is going to take a different path, a different approach than mine. It will depend on how she interprets the signals she receives from God as I explain them to her."

"You're going to try and convert her to your way of thinking?"

"I'm going to explain my mission here, the calling I've received from my father, and let her make the decision whether she wants to be a follower or not."

"A follower?"

"Yes."

"As a follower, what will be required of her?"

"I don't know exactly, James. I hope she won't be asked to follow me to the grave, but there are those who will. You may be one of those, James..."

It was as if James had been suddenly smacked between the eyes with a ball peen hammer very hard.

He hardly heard what Jesse said next: "I'm glad that your feelings about Mary Alice have changed. She's not a bad person. She has simply not been given a proper chance to be good."

Chapter 32

Houston-Barrett Construction in Peril

TED BARRETT AND Jerrod Houston had another clandestine meeting at a mutually agreeable location, unknown to most, a little used swap shop gathering late in the afternoon when most buyers and sellers had left. They huddled together and attempted to look as inconspicuous as possible while scanning articles for sale with no intent to buy. Surprisingly, Ted was doing a good job of disguising his temperament, which was at or near the blastoff point, such as when objects powered by incredible doses of high-octane jet fuel leave earth's atmosphere and travel into space, sometimes never to be seen again.

"So you're telling me that your well-laid-out plan failed again?"

"Yes, it did unfortunately, and the worst is yet to come."

"What do you mean?"

"I mean, Ted, that the sheriff and his team of deputies are hot on my trail. I can't turn around without bumping into one of them."

"So obviously, that means that we need to forget about dispatching Isaac, our chief nemesis, at present anyway?"

"More like forever."

"Why forever?"

"Because it was attempted murder, Ted. Things like that don't go unnoticed anymore like they did in the wild west. We have law and order now. People who commit crimes are caught and punished."

"You don't say? You don't need to talk down to me, Jerrod. I understand the gravity of the situation. The question is, what do we do now? We still need to establish ourselves in the suburbs and do so quickly. If we don't, then our next step will be to liquidate our assets as soon as possible and count our losses or else file for bankruptcy. I say liquidate our assets, but we have no assets that aren't tied to securities of one form or another, mostly bank loans."

"I get you, Ted. I wish I didn't, but I do understand. The problem is that our hands are tied now. We can't do anything without the suspicion of guilt being pointed squarely at us."

"Okay, we're in desperate straits or hot water, whatever you want to call it. There has got to be a fail-safe option in the middle of this dilemma, Jerrod. I know you've thought this thing through in case something goes wrong, and it did. Now tell me what our next option is, and don't say 'I don't know.' Let's be adult about this thing and come up with a workable solution. Let's not just jump in the water and drown, like a couple of idiots that can't see the forest for the trees and give up, never to be seen again."

Jerrod stared at the face of the other without speaking until finally, he voiced the obvious: "The only chance we've got is to try and discredit Isaac and his family, Tom, like I've mentioned before, and I don't see us getting very far with that notion because, quite frankly, we're the ones who've been discredited so far. Isaac and his family have taken everything we've thrown at them and managed to stay afloat. They are on schedule with their construction project and are doing quality work. The only chance we have is to try and smear the man with references to the boy, Jesse. That's our only chance, as I see it and to date, that hasn't gotten off the ground."

"Then we need to step up our smear campaign, don't we?"

"Sure, and in the process, I'm dodging the sheriff and his crew who are looking at me through a microscope to the point that I can't even turn around without having to answer for myself."

Ted thought long and hard before replying, "Your daughter, Mary Alice, and the boy Jesse are seeing each other, aren't they?"

"Yes. What about it?"

"Would she be willing to plead our case for us?"

"What do you mean?"

He looked around to make sure no one had come close. "Would she be willing to cry 'rape,' or something to that effect, claim that she has been seduced, anything to get others thinking that Isaac and his family are really the guilty party?"

Jerrod thought it out carefully. "Perhaps. It's worth a try anyway. Right now, we don't have much of an alternative. We're dead in the water without a paddle."

"Hey, we've been there before, haven't we? I remember when we started this team. We didn't hardly have a dollar to our name, but we made it work, didn't we? We were just back from Nam and had a shiny war record and not much else and bought the confidence of important people to the point that they were willing to stick out their necks for us. We've got to do the same thing now, Jerrod. It's time to show the opposition just how much we learned in the jungles of Vietnam. Let's get dirty again like we did there and make it happen. We're fighters, aren't we? Then let's fight."

"I'm not sure, Ted. The situation is different now. We're the bad guys right now, not the guys with the shiny brass buttons and military presence. But I agree with you, we need to fight. This may be our only chance. I will talk to Mary and see if she's willing to do this for us. She hasn't been willing to do anything so far but tell me how great he is. It's nauseous."

"Maybe you can use her in an underhanded way. Try a bribe, only don't tell her what it is you're attempting to do."

"I've tried that tact already. It doesn't work. She's convinced she's being asked to work for the wrong side."

"Well, whose daughter is she anyway? Force her hand a little. This isn't tidily winks after all. We're fighting for our lives unless you want to go down without a fight."

"I'm with you, Ted. We're going to win this thing."

"Great! Keep me posted."

"I will."

Chapter 33

Criminology at Work

ROY COLLIER WAS Tom Behrenger's chief forensics' officer and doubled also as strategist and as clerk of sorts. In other words, he was versatile and invaluable since he had thirty-one years of experience in hard-nosed law enforcement work from the ground up. Sixty-one years of age with a short, bushy gray mustache and receding hairline that covered what little hair he had left on top, he had started as a deputy sheriff and continued in that line for seven years before being classified as detective. From there, he had worked at several different positions until becoming sheriff, serving for six years before retiring early to enjoy family life. When his three children left home and when Tom Behrenger became sheriff, he had coaxed Roy out of retirement so that he could utilize his expertise in the office, doing research on special projects. Thus, he had gotten the assignment to analyze the nineteen individuals that Isaac Christian had picked out as possible suspects in the shooting incident that killed Isaac but not really since he wasn't dead. It was still a little hard to understand what happened in that matter. That was why Roy's job with the sheriff's office was so engaging, why he had decided ultimately to come back and dive right back into the thick of things. You never knew what it was that you might uncover that would become pivotal in the final analysis or how life became logical in such an illogical world through research.

After hours and hours of background checks, Roy had narrowed the nineteen subjects to what he called his final five. From that list, he had studied four out of the five suspects carefully, beginning with family, job experience, attachment to special interest groups—including politics—and of course, their personal file of warrants or arrests issued or made, along with any abridgment of the law that was part of that record, however small or large, that hadn't been resolved in timely fashion. None of the four had any situational discrepancies with the law that amounted to what might be considered leading, or confrontational, or even of a questionable nature, so he had dismissed them.

In turning to the fifth individual of the group, an individual named Sydney Ventura, the initial background check had been virtually the same, an individual without any blemishes or scrapes with the law, someone who appeared to be in perfect harmony with societal norms in all respects.

He was an individual without a record of family life, he noted, and that was usually a red flag, an indication to look deeper into childhood and young adult behavior patterns. He found that the youth had been raised in an orphanage until he was sixteen, when he joined the military. That was interesting because he hadn't been of eligible enrollment age. He peered deeper. His military record had been spotless. He had received a Meritorious Service Award when his initial enrollment period had ended. Following that, he reenlisted and served an additional four years. He had achieved the rank of sergeant and received another Meritorious Service Award. He was, it seemed, an excellent soldier.

When his second tour of duty had ended, he was picked up by a select military service group and had served with them for a full term of duty, most of that time in Vietnam, and achieved the rank of master sergeant. It was there that he had received a Purple Heart as commendation for extraordinary service above or beyond the call of duty. He researched further and found out that he had gone into an enemy encampment and saved his commanding officer, who was being held captive. Both men had been injured but not critically and had returned to duty.

He found the military history of the man compelling and continued to research. His commanding officer at the time had been an individual named Jerrod Houston. That name sounded familiar. He reread the full record of the shooting of Isaac Christian and following investigation and found out that Jerrod Houston had been named as the chief suspect in the shooting but, during interrogation, had provided substantial proof that he wasn't at the scene of the shooting. Things were started to fit together.

He researched Sydney Ventura's career as a special forces officer and found out that the man was classified expert as a marksman, especially with a bolt action rifle, the military version of a .30-06, and had been used extensively as a sniper. He had been in a platoon commanded at one time by a lieutenant named Ted Barrett. That name had been mentioned earlier in a briefing, he recalled. He did some more digging and found out that Tom Barrett and Jerrod Houston were the principal owners of Houston-Barrett Construction, a huge construction company operating principally in the more populous area of the state.

Roy Collier was better than a bloodhound when he was on the trail of a felon. He researched the background of Houston-Barrett Construction and found out that the company, though at one time a highly solvent entity, had experienced tremendous financial losses recently and was badly insolvent. At present, they were being threatened with loan forfeiture proceedings, a takeover of all assets and securities by their various lending institutions, banks, etc. The chief competition the giant construction company had faced recently had been a one-man construction company named Isaac Christian Custom Building. It all suddenly made sense. The caption describing the Christian company read, "I'll build you a palace fit for a king and queen."

Recognizing the wartime relationship between Sydney Ventura, Jerrod Houston, and Ted Barrett, Roy dug up all the information he could find on Ventura, who stuck out now as the triggerman in the shooting. He found out very little since the man had been released from military duty. In fact, there was nothing at all, except for one statement in the paper following his release from active duty as a special forces officer.

In a column in a local paper, a reporter, a man who had interviewed the military hero for such he was, had asked Ventura what he thought he would do since he would no longer be in the military. He had laughingly replied, "I'll probably find a place to hide so that no one can find me. I've made a few enemies, and sometimes it's hard to forget." Apparently, the man had done just that, found a place to hide and was still hiding, vanished from the face of the earth, except when duty called…

Armed with the information he had been able to uncover, Roy Collier asked for a meeting with Tom Behrenger. "Sheriff, I've got something to show you…"

When he had finished, the sheriff beamed and said, "Okay, how are we going to find Sydney Ventura?"

"I've got just one thought," the investigator replied. "I don't think he's anywhere in the United States."

"Then where is he? We've got to find the guy."

"I would ask Jerrod Houston or Ted Barrett. They would know. They hired him to do a job."

Chapter 34

A New Problem for Anne Maria

IT WAS EVENING. The family had eaten, and Jesse was helping his mother put away eating and cooking utensils that had been washed and dried by hand. They were alone in the kitchen at the time, and others had assembled in the living room to find entertainment on the television, currently in the middle of the evening news broadcast. She was glad for the chance to talk alone.

He had recently commented that the new home he and James had been working on was nearly finished and that it would be time for him to make some changes in his life. That statement had alarmed her greatly for it hinted of a time when he would be leaving, and she was afraid that it might be for good.

"You talked about leaving, son," she began. "I hadn't thought it would be so soon. There's still so much to do here at home."

He nodded but didn't say anything.

"Isaac is still recovering from the shooting," she offered. "He still needs a lot of help before he'll be able to go back to work."

"I know, Mom."

"Then how can you talk of leaving us when we need your help so badly?"

He put away a couple of cooking pans and turned to look at her squarely. "It's nearly time that I start doing that which I promised my father I would do," he said simply.

"But what can we do without you, son? You need to consider us as well."

"I know," he affirmed, placing an arm around her, "but James has proven that he can do all that needs to be done in the construction business until Dad returns. He is very capable, believe me. Then, when Dad returns, James may decide to follow me. We've talked somewhat and he is seeing things through my eyes more and more. I haven't asked him to follow me, but I think that he will eventually."

She was devastated but tried bravely to hide her disappointment. "What about the others?" she asked.

"What do you mean, Mother?"

"What about me? What about the other children besides James. What's going to happen to us when you're gone?"

He continued to keep his arm around her waist and gazed into her eyes. "You and Dad will be fine," he offered, smiling. "You did just fine before I came along, and you've been wonderful parents for each of us, training us up to be as capable as you are. You will be blessed to be able to continue to do a great work here, at home."

"But the younger children need you, Jesse."

"I will always be near them. I don't intend to forget about my brothers and sisters, but, Mother, I have other brothers and sisters that need me as well."

She looked down and nodded. "I'm sorry, son. I had forgotten."

"In time, some or perhaps even all of the younger children will make a decision to follow me as James will do. I won't try and persuade them one way or the other. It's something they will have to decide for themselves."

"Oh, son, it's so scary to think about. I'm afraid of losing—"

"No one loses, Mother, when we put Heavenly Father first. We may lose an earthly contest or two, such as what has happened to Dad, but Heavenly Father will reward all who choose to follow him. That is his promise to the faithful."

"I know, son. I know, but it is difficult, especially when we are called to give up that which is so dear to us. What will you do about Mary Alice? Will you leave her also?"

"Mary Alice and I haven't talked about long-term relations, Mother. We've made no promises to each other. She knows that I'll be leaving at some point, and I believe she's all right with that. I won't ask her to follow me if that's what you mean."

"I guess it is. I was just wondering about how much you had shared with her, about Father, and all that that would encompass in time. She's been such an unbeliever before meeting you."

"I know, Mom. She has changed dramatically, however. I'm not condemning her for things that happened in the past. I have come to save people from their sins, whatever they happen to be, and to give them new life. That is what I'm all about, and it means that Mary Alice can have a new life, too, just like the others. She's a sweet person underneath all that has happened before, and she's beginning to develop a belief in God."

"Do you love her then?"

"I do, Mother, just like I love you and Dad and James and the other children. She is my sister after all."

"Oh, Jesse, I'm going to miss you so much." She wiped away a tear and then another and then broke down and cried. "I don't want you to leave, son."

"I know but I must. And, Mother, it won't be for a time yet. I still have things to do to prepare for leaving. I've got more questions that will have to be resolved with Father. He will be the one to decide for me when it is time to go. It's not something that I will determine, believe me. My life, my talents, my energy, and all that I aspire to do are carefully determined by him. He will prepare each of us for that eventuality."

"All right, son. You promise me that you won't go until he says it is time?"

"I promise, Mom."

Chapter 35

Another Subterfuge

MARY ALICE HAD finished up an online math assignment and was preparing to get ready for bed when her father knocked on her bedroom door and entered quietly.

"Can we talk for a few minutes?" he asked, settling in at the foot of her bed.

"Sure, Dad, what's up?"

He knew she would be tired and anxious to go to bed and so he didn't mince words. "You know how I asked you to help me with Jesse and the Christian family? I asked you to become more familiar with Jesse especially because of all the slander concerning him."

"Yeah, I remember. And I tried, Dad. But it just didn't work out very well. I think I told you, the more I've found out about the family—particularly about Jesse—the more I've come to admire them."

"Well, things have come to a head in the construction business, Mary. The Houston-Barrett Construction Company is experiencing a terrible downfall in business since we've moved our chief operations to this area."

"Okay, and so has Isaac and his business had their challenges, especially since the shooting, but they seem to keep going anyway. Can't Houston-Barrett do the same?"

"It's different with us. We're a huge contracting business with an extraordinarily large overhead that needs to be fed. Isaac Christian

Custom Building is a small business with little overhead. They operate largely on a cash basis without entanglements that need to be addressed, such as hefty payroll and subcontractors that demand our cooperation and a percentage of our assets in order to be able to remain ready for new and future business opportunities."

"So? But you've always had these burdens to carry, Dad. What is so different about now?"

He shuffled his position on the bed, suddenly uncomfortable. "As I said, Mary, we've moved our chief operations to this area. It hasn't been a good move. We anticipated that the area would boom. It hasn't, though it will probably do so in the future. Meanwhile, we're being undercut here by Christian's contracting business. He has got a monopoly on construction projects in this area. He can build for considerably less than we can and is noted for quality work. He's a good deal slower than us but makes folks happy because of the final product. As a result, we're plunging into serious indebtedness because we can't service our lenders, the banks, etc. that have pledged money to keep us rolling. It's getting very critical unfortunately, to the point that we may not be able to operate much longer unless the situation changes dramatically."

Mary Alice, concerned but also knowing something of what had transpired to date concerning attempts to put the company's chief adversary out of business, sat down near him on the bed and turned to confront him. "And so we put out a contract on Isaac Christian. We attempt to murder the man so that his business will die as well. But it hasn't happened, has it? Christian survived, and now the two oldest sons are picking up where the dad left off. Shall we put out a contract on them as well? What about it, Dad? Shall we attempt to murder Jesse and James as well?"

"Mary, I knew I shouldn't talk to you about this. I'm crazy for doing so, but I thought you might consider helping Mom and I at this time, when we need your help so badly. Excuse me for trying. I almost forgot that you are our daughter and owe us for all the years we've supported your outlandish lifestyle, attempting to make things right when you tried so hard to destroy the family image." He stood up and turned to leave.

"Dad...I'm sorry. I know I owe you and Mom a good deal for putting up with me in my craziness when wrong seemed right and right seemed wrong. I was totally mixed up, but, Dad, in many respects, I was the girl that you and Mom made me out to be. You threw me at the opposite sex. You used me to allure others to partner with you in business deals. I never knew anything else than playing the coquette and sleeping around when nothing else worked. I helped make your business, Dad, and frankly it has cost me a life of my own when I could have become something other than a fixture, something to be used and discarded." She was red-faced and angry with tears spouting like raindrops that couldn't be controlled.

He let her cry and then put his arm around her. "I'm sorry, Mary. If you will help me this one last time, I won't ask you anymore, I promise."

"What is it you want me to do?"

He wiped her face with his handkerchief and tried to calm his beleaguered nerves. "I want you to make it public that Jesse has raped you. That will be a start to an effective smear campaign that will hopefully put Christian Custom Building out of business."

She nearly shot off the bed, a cannonball erupted. "He has never even kissed me, Dad!"

"That's all right. It doesn't have to be the truth, Mary. We just need to get people to believe that he is a letch. Do you understand?"

"*A letch?*"

"Yes, someone who is given to lechery. A person who preys on young women, or young men, whatever happens to be available."

She stared at him through narrowed eyelids. "No, Dad. I won't do that, not in a million years. Jesse is no more a letch than you're Houdini, or Abraham Lincoln, or even God. I would die before I would make a statement like that."

He spoke calmly, "That's too bad, Mary, because that's what I'm planning on doing, making a statement to that effect and attributing it to you. People will believe it because it reflects on you, and they know your history," and he turned and left.

Chapter 36

A Shooter and a Target

ROY COLLIER AND Tom Behrenger were together at the snack room at the sheriff's office. The conversation quite naturally turned to the attempted murder of Isaac Christian.

"So," the sheriff said, "we've implicated the three soldiers in grand style, thanks to you. We think we know who the shooter was, of the three, and that the other two put him up to it because of the desperate financial condition that Houston-Barrett Construction is in currently. Sydney Ventura is the odd man out because he doesn't fit in the picture other than the fact that he is a close friend who proved his friendship in the military by dint of being a crack shot with a rifle."

"Yes. Without question. What we've got to do now is find some hard evidence to prove our assumptions."

The sheriff nodded. "That's always the hard part, isn't it?"

"Yes, of course. Let's start with what we know. I've been doing all I can to find out information about Ventura. The man is a ghost who doesn't really exist, on paper anyway, but rumor has it that he is a legitimate hit man, a full-time sniper who has struck many times but who can't be implicated in any of the coincidences of sniper fire because he is so very elusive. He has earned the nickname 'Air Raid' because he flies from here to there and can't be detected. This all comes from the rumor mill, mind you, but I have the feeling that it's true."

"So if he's so elusive, how is it that people can contact him when he takes on a hit job—supposing that he is, indeed, a full-fledged hit man."

"That's the rub, all right. I can't come to grips with it, except to say the man must have a contact person that sets up his operations, an agent if you will."

"That sounds reasonable," the sheriff agreed, "and if so, it would probably be one of the two men that know the most about him and who would be willing to feed his ego, namely Jerrod Houston or Ted Barrett, because of the ultra-close relationship they enjoyed in the military."

"Exactly."

"All right then, let's proceed on that premise. I've already established a wiretap for both men, so we're good on that end. What else can we do?"

"I will continue to try and find out more about Ventura. We can do the same for the other two, attempt to find out more about their relationship in the military. I've got a feeling we're missing something important."

"Like what, Roy?"

"I'm not sure, maybe something of a family nature. I need to check out possible extended family tie-ins. We don't know anything about Ventura's parents, of course, but I need to do more checking on the other two."

"Okay. Are we ready to make an arrest?"

"I wouldn't advise it yet. The two construction magnates are legends because of their history as special forces heroes as is Syd Ventura. The two corporate men have very capable lawyers who know the business of law backward and forwards. They wouldn't be in custody fifteen minutes if we arrested them, probably without bail even being set."

"What else can we legitimately do? Oh, wait, I've got an idea!"

"What is it?"

"What if we try and lure Ventura out of hiding? Say, create a situation that is enticing enough to grab his attention and then set a trap and watch how he responds. If we work our cards right, we might even get him to open up about the others."

"It's far out, but I'll give it some thought. Have you got any other suggestions?"

The sheriff thought for a few moments, slurping his coffee over his chin in the process. "Let's suppose that either Ted Barrett or Jerrod Houston is the agent you talked about, the person who sets up Ventura for action. Both men are scratching the bottom of the barrel for money right now in deep financial trouble. The attempted murder of Joseph Christian went south badly. Who made the payment for that one, or in fact, was payment actually made? I would guess that a professional hit job would cost around seventy-five to a hundred grand or more. Let's check the balance sheet on their banking ledger and see if anything like that shows up. But also, suppose that payment hasn't been made yet. If we could set up some kind of scenario again where we could lure the shooter out of his hiding place— say, promise of payment or even say, a rich payoff of a wealthy client, something of that nature—we could nab him in the process, maybe even all three."

"It's iffy, very iffy. First off, I think that we've got to establish which of the two men is the agent for Ventura. If so—and I think we're on the right track there—that person has to know how to contact him. Let's take your idea and set up a fake situation where Ventura needs to be contacted and then attempt to intercept that contact message. That may tell us where Ventura is, and we can proceed from there."

"All right. Let's work on that, but remember, we're tracking two desperate men—and a third we're not sure of—who have shown a tendency to go off like a couple of nuclear reactors, meltdown and all."

"Right."

Chapter 37

A Classic Confrontation

JESSE WAS CONFLICTED after talking with his mother, realizing there was strong feeling in the family that he needed to stay home a while longer before leaving to serve his father. He spoke with James and told him that he would be absent from the construction site the following day and to proceed without him. He got up early the next morning, dressed, and left the home without eating, planning to be gone for a full day but no longer. He took no water with him, feeling a need to feed his spirit rather than his body.

He walked a distance away from the outlying community toward the hills in the background, an area he had frequented before. Reaching the hills, he could see a prominent high point beyond, a spectacular spot that overreached the lower-lying hills. He felt a need to isolate himself on that point and continued walking.

Reaching the base of the high point or illy crafted steeple, it became immediately apparent that it would be difficult to ascend the cliff-like sides of the spiraling pinnacle. Undaunted, he looked for and found what he considered to be a way up the side of the high mound and carefully began ascending toward the top. It took considerably more time to execute the climb that he had anticipated as it turned out, and he found himself tired and hurting as he finally reached the top, his arm muscles particularly strained from having to pull himself up to gain leverage with his feet.

The view from the top was worth the effort, he reasoned, and he found a suitable spot on a flat rock where he could sit down and enjoy the broad, sunlit expanse below him. That lasted for several minutes and then the effects of the stringent climb and the warm sun played upon him until he became drowsy and began to give in to the notion of napping a short time. He stretched out and eased into a more comfortable position on his rock undercarriage and soon fell asleep.

As he napped, he dreamed that he was on a lofty crest of a mountain, far from any hint of civilization. Suddenly a ghoulish demon appeared and challenged him, saying he was king of the surrounding mountains and that no one else was allowed on his domain.

The fiend was so devilish that Jesse felt fear stab at him like a saber thrust but gained courage and replied, "God made these mountains and valleys and gave man dominion over them. I am the *Son of Man*, and can rule over you if you wish to contend with me."

The demon pondered what had been said and retaliated, "Maybe God did make the earth, but the riches of eternity belong to me. If you will bow down and worship me, I will share my riches with you."

"I have all the riches I need," Jesse apprized the fiery demon. "You have nothing at all that would interest me."

"Oh no," he quickly retorted. "I have a troupe of beautiful women, the loveliest that man can behold, and they are at my command. Shall I call for them to please you? Whatever you wish is their desire."

"I find my pleasure in serving my God," Jesse countered. "You can keep your harem to yourself if that's what pleases you."

The demon persisted: "You are tired and hungry. You have no water. I can call up a feast for the two of us that will satisfy the most ardent traveler. It will be yours now at this instant if you wish."

"No thanks, Mr. Ghoul, I will starve my body a little longer and then God and I will have a feast together, a spiritual feast that is."

"You're no fun at all, you know. I can surround you with all the comforts devised by man to please the body, and here you are, starving yourself, sleeping on a rock with nothing but the dull earth to recommend you."

Jesse smiled. "I know you. I know all your tricks too. I know that you are a master at telling lies, so good at sophistry that you can't tell the truth from error. You use your lies to deceive others. I want no part in your games, demon ghoul. Be gone from me! I want nothing to do with you."

The demon left in great anguish, gnashing his teeth together, and Jesse was able to relax a bit and enjoy his respite for a change. It wasn't long, however, before he conjured up another scene. It was his earthly family, and they came close and hugged and kissed him on his face and hands, saying how much they loved him and were worried that he might have left without telling them of his departure.

"I'm still with you," he told them. "I haven't gone anywhere, except to visit with my father."

In his mind, Isaac stepped forward and called out, "My boy, my health isn't nearly as good as it needs to be. I still need you to help with the construction projects. James is coming along, but both he and I need your help and need it badly. I pray that you will heed what it is that I have to say. I love you, Jesse. Thanks for all you've done for each of us. Please come back."

After Isaac had kissed him on the cheek and shed a tear with him, his mother began to speak: "Son, I've been praying to Father that we could have more time together, and I feel like he has given assurance that it will be so as I wish. I can't bear the thought of your leaving. If you leave, son, I'm afraid you will never return. Please stay until the younger children are older anyway."

She had just finished crying at his feet when James stepped forward and exclaimed, "Jesse, I can't do what it is that you can do. I need more training. You must return and give me the help that I need, or all will be lost with the family. Please don't desert the family, Jesse. Remember us and remember Mary Alice. She needs your help too, just as we do."

Suddenly, Mary Alice appeared in the family throng and rushed to him, arms extended. "I love you, Jesse," she called out tearfully. "I thought I could be okay with your leaving, but I find that I can't,

Jesse, I can't. You must return and help me deal with my father. He says I must help him attempt to destroy you and the family. I don't know what to do, Jesse. I must have your help to be able to resist him." She also knelt at his feet and cried mournfully, "Please help me, Jesse. I love you so much."

Last of all, Jeri came forward, speaking for the younger children, tears in her eyes, and said, "Jesse, I have no one to hold my hand. You must come back and hold my hand, or I fear that I will perish. Please come back, Jesse, for me and for the others. We need you badly."

Jesse's mind came back to the rational world, his eyes watery, and looked around. There was darkness everywhere. He had been on the crest of the natural steeple all day and into the night. He was cold and alone.

He began to pray, "Dear God, my Father, help me know thy will. When it is time, when I can serve you with all my heart, when I can be of most service to all of thy precious sons and daughters everywhere, help me have the strength to pursue my earthly mission to the end, whatever is required of me, I pray…"

With the dawn of the new day, he returned home to wait for the call, when it would be time for him to leave. It would be soon, he felt. He also understood that more would be expected of him at home. Emotions were running high, so very high…

Chapter 38

Insinuations Circulate Widely

IN THE VERY next edition of the local paper, *The New Herald*, in the editorial section, the following was published:

> *I wish to thank the people of this small community who have welcomed the Houston-Barrett Construction company and given us reason to hope that our stay here can be lengthy and profitable for each of us. We wish to build homes of value for you and for your children in the years to come. Our company has a reputation of building fine, quality homes that can grace any neighborhood, and we are pleased that we can share that virtue with you.*
>
> *Recently, my daughter was attacked on the street as she came to the post office. Three overzealous girls attacked her and nearly ended her life. They claimed that she was a misfit of sorts, someone unwelcome here. She and I have talked about the incident. We harbor no ill feeling toward anyone in this community including those three girls.*
>
> *They accused my daughter of being amoral to the point that she has no respect for her God-given body. That is not true. She has respect for God, for*

God's teachings, and for her body. She has deter-mined to learn more about God and to be com-pletely free of accusations such as those hurled at her by the girls in question.

Now she has been attacked again. This time it has happened under the pretense of a meaningful relationship introduced by the son of Isaac Christian, a local contractor who is well-known in the commu-nity. The boy in question, Jesse Christian, attempted to rape my daughter. By the grace of God, she was saved from that assault, but the family fears that it may happen again.

I have thought to make public these attacks and call for community support to ensure that such things don't happen to my daughter or to anyone else. We love our home and community. We need your support and your love to make sure that we can live together in tranquility and love.

Best regards, Jerrod Houston, Co-Partner, Houston-Barrett Construction Company

In the week succeeding that publication, the following was found in the editorial section of the same community newspaper:

My name is Mary Alice Houston. I am the same who was introduced as having been attacked twice separately, the second attack including an attempted rape as alleged by my father, Jerrod Houston of Houston-Barrett Construction Company, in the editorial section last week.

It is true that I was attacked by three girls while going to the post office. I was also saved from severe injury during that attack by Jesse Christian, who seeing that some action was necessary, stepped in and stopped the fight.

My father has seen fit to charge Mr. Christian with assault, claiming that in a separate attack he attempted to rape me. That is not correct. He has done no such thing. If it had happened, it would have been reported to the local police. I assure you, no such thing happened.

My father has his own agenda about why he intends to discredit Jesse Christian and his family. I will leave that to him and to others who may have a more complete understanding of this whole affair. I wish that I wasn't a pawn, someone to be used to provoke others to a result that would please Houston-Barrett Construction Company.

What was mentioned about my character in passing by my father is unfortunately true. I have made mistakes in the past that have colored my character. It is my desire to move past those mistakes and present myself as a young woman of high moral character. I am working toward that end. I should add that Jesse Christian is helping me in that respect. He has taught me how to have greater respect for my body and for others as well.

Please take note of what I have to say: Jesse Christian and his family have done nothing to deserve the insinuation that has come to light through the comments of my father.

Most sincerely, Mary Alice Houston.

Chapter 39

A Desperate Move

WITH GREAT EXPEDIENCE, Jerrod Houston and Ted Barrett found a time and place where they could meet. The conversation was spiced with insinuations, directed mostly at Jerrod, though he was, in turn, quick to defend himself.

"I'm at wit's end, Ted. What am I supposed to do? My daughter cares more for Jesse Christian and his family than she does for me, for our family, who gave her everything she wanted as a youth until there was no more to give. She has been a virtual sponge bursting at the seams but unwilling to give back."

"That's your problem, Jerrod. You raised her wrong, that's plain to see. The problem is, what are we going to do about it now, now that she has made the two of us look like fools?"

"I'm ready to try anything. I've got to do something that will shut her mouth. That much is apparent."

"I can shut her mouth," Barrett boasted.

"Oh, sure, and why don't you phone the police and tell them what it is you plan to do for they will surely know without asking."

"I guess you're right, but you're the one who said we've got to put a lid on her lip. What do you have in mind that hasn't already been tried? None of your crackpot schemes have worked so far. You might as well make it a trifecta."

"That's not funny, Ted. Now look, we're not getting anywhere by bickering with each other. Let's get serious and figure out a way to save face with the community and with our lenders because if we don't, we're going to be out of business. Not only that, but we're also going to be headed for prison for a very long stay, maybe even for the gas chamber."

"That's the first thing you've said that has a sense of credibility to it. Here's what I propose…"

Chapter 40

Check or Checkmate?

IT DIDN'T TAKE Roy Collier and Tom Behrenger long to meet and go over the activities of the past few days, especially the two editorials that had been published.

"There's trouble in River City," Tom said, parroting Robert Preston from Meredith Wilson's *The Music Man*, a play long since forgotten by most.

Behrenger was a keen advocate of old Broadway plays and enjoyed drawing on those memories occasionally. They had been studying the two editorials that had been published in the community paper and had just received a report from the two detectives that had been following Jerrod Houston and Ted Barrett, Vincent Abrams and Jake Forsyth, reporting on their quickly arranged meeting of the night before.

"Did they have anything interesting to report?" Collier asked.

"Only that the two men met and that the conversation was hot and heavy. They didn't hear any of what was said but reported that both men were highly agitated and irritable."

"That sounds reasonable. Their multimillion-dollar business is going down the drain and quickly."

"What's your take?" Roy inquired. "They've got their backs against the wall, and the firing squad is loaded and ready to shoot. What's going to be their response?"

"The men are both fighters. They've been in the trenches before. They'll fight all right, and I'm worried that it's going to get even uglier."

"Who's going to be the target this time? And will they attempt to use Ventura, or will they handle it themselves?"

"I'm thinking they'll contact Ventura. This is his kind of parade after all. He seems to like it when the stakes are the highest. My guess is that they'll hit someone from the Christian family—not Isaac but someone else, maybe Jesse or both Jesse and James, who are handling all the construction work now."

"That's not smart. Surely they know that it will reflect directly on them if something happens to either Isaac Christian or his sons."

"They know and it does present a problem. They've got to somehow get Mary Alice to stop talking about how great the Christian family is and, at the same time, squash Christian and his construction firm. I think…" He started but didn't finish. Instead, he looked up and away, like he was staring at something invisible but highly imaginative. "That's it!" he finally said.

"What's it? You're way ahead of me, Tom."

"I think I know what they're going to do," he erupted, pleased with himself.

"Please tell me. I'm all eyes and ears. You've got a captive audience."

"It makes sense. They're going to hit Mary Alice and then pin her death on Jesse or the Christian family. That way, they kill two birds with one stone."

"That's brilliant but kill Mary Alice? She's Jerrod Houston's daughter, remember?"

"Yes, she certainly is, and she's also the wedge between the Houston-Barrett Construction Company and Christian Custom Building. Don't you see, she's got to go if Houston-Barrett is going to survive?"

"I agree, but isn't there something else that can be done short of putting out a contract on her, a contract ordered by her own father?"

"All right, tell me what else they could do."

"They could…" But he simply couldn't think of anything else that could work nearly as effectively. "That's got to be the answer," he finally conceded, "but how are they going to manage to do the job and then pin the blame on the family?"

"First off," he countered, "the job is going to have to happen at or near the Christian's construction site, probably on-site I would guess."

"Okay, I agree."

"And because it takes place on-site, they can come up with an imaginative way to accuse someone from their family of her death, probably Jesse, since he and she are thick now."

Roy thought ahead. "Do you think that Sydney Ventura would agree to put a hit on a young woman, especially someone who rivals the physical presence and glamour of any beauty queen most of us have ever laid eyes on, or hope to see, in our lifetimes?"

"That might be laying it on a little thick, but yes, I think Sydney Ventura would do just about anything that Houston-Barrett asked him to do based on the relationship they've enjoyed in the past."

"Wow is all I can say. What a waste of beautiful flesh."

"Now, Roy, you're getting a bit too personal about this whole thing."

"Hey, I'm an old person, and you only get to see a few perfect women. You know what I mean. She's gorgeous. If I were her father, I'd be hiring a bodyguard to make sure nothing ever happened to her…"

He nodded and smiled. "Well, we're simply surmising, but I feel like we may have hit on the only solution that Houston-Barrett could possibly invent to be able to stay in the game."

"I'm afraid I agree with you. Let me add something else."

"What is it?"

"It's far out, but it might simply be genuine."

"Explain yourself."

"I get a few copies of national papers that I read to stay up with news of importance around the world, along with editorials that provide insight, both pro and con."

"Go ahead."

"I glanced at a highly circulated New York paper yesterday and in the 'Want Ad' section. I found something terribly curious."

"What was it?"

"I found this." He produced a short want ad that read, "Have trouble with a pest? We take care of pests. Call for more information."

"That does sound strange. Was there a number to call?"

"There was."

"Did you call the number?"

"I did."

"And?"

"I listened to a recording that explained in short detail how a pest can destroy homelife, both inside and outside the home, and how infectious such beasts can be and then finished with a curious statement."

"What was the statement?"

"If your goal is complete eradiation of the harmful pest, leave a number and we will contact you."

"Did you leave a number?"

"I didn't. I wasn't sure I should expose myself in that manner. What do you think?"

"I think you should invite them to contact you by giving a number that's totally clean and then let's see what happens."

"All right. I do think, however, that we should attempt to place a trace on the caller, if you agree?"

"I agree, totally."

"It's far out, as I said, but it might be the contact person for Sydney Ventura. Could we possibly be so lucky?"

"Let's hope so."

Chapter 41

Anne Looks Ahead

ANNE MARIA WAS in between jobs, a rare occurrence for her, something she hadn't experienced since she couldn't remember when. She was weary and needed a moment to catch her breath. The actions of several weeks had finally caught up with her to the point that she was hardly capable of reviving herself no matter what. It was futile to even attempt to rejuvenate herself, she feared.

She was wearied from being a home nurse to Isaac, taking upon herself his responsibilities as well as her own and attending to his medical contingencies, all of which were a good deal more demanding than there was time in the day, almost. She was weary of the responsibility of homeschooling the children, having to develop lesson plans for each of them because of their variance in ages and tailor those lessons to the whole, making them interesting and informative and challenging to each in order to retain interest and excitement in learning for all.

She was weary in worrying about Jesse, the Anointed One, and what lie in store for him; in what manner and substance and time she was to assist in helping him elevate himself to the highest potential for greatness, as was to be his calling. She wearied herself in worrying that he would leave and not be prepared for that calling or that he would not leave and fail. She couldn't help but worry about his relationship with Mary Alice and how that relationship would develop, or not, and whether it would be a deterrent to his calling. She worried about Mary Alice's family, especially her father and what he could do for it seemed most apparent that he was the one who was responsible for the attempted murder of her husband.

She was also weary from carrying the normal everyday burdens that a mother takes upon herself, the preparing of meals, the cleaning chores that never stopped, and all that was to be done to make sure that each of the children had clothes to wear that suited the occasion and adequate for each job they were undertaking and much more that only a mother of five children could fully understand: be a nurse, a psychologist, a fortune teller, a Mother Teresa of sorts.

Recently, in planning lessons for the children, she had put together a unit on English literature which had been warmly received by the older ones and rewarding not only to the children but also to her in the sense that she learned how great men and women, noted poets and philosophers, had overcome tremendous odds in becoming great. An example of that was the poet John Keats from the Romantic era of poets, including Wordsworth, Coleridge, and Shelley, as well as others.

Keats was the one who stood out most for her as an individual who had overcome great personal challenges. Orphaned at sixteen years of age because of the deaths of his mother and brother to tuberculosis, he had gone forward and received schooling that led to a certificate or license to be a doctor. Although licensed in that respect, his wish was to become a poet of renown, and he had ultimately given up all to follow that strong desire.

Keats published his first book of poems at age twenty-two. From that point, he continued to write extensively, publishing such great poems as "The Eve of St. Agnes" and "Ode on a Grecian Urn." As a result, he had become one of the major poets of his time. It was also during this time that he became a victim of tuberculosis, the same disease that had claimed the lives of his other family members. He died at age twenty-five, never having never been married, alone, and disconsolate as felt in his poem, "When I Have Fears That I May Cease to Be," written in 1818 at twenty-two years of age.

When I have fears that I may cease to be
Before my pen has gleaned my teeming brain,
Before high-piled books in charactery
Hold like rich garners the full-ripened grain;
When I behold, upon the night's starred face,
Huge cloudy symbols of a high romance,
And think that I may never live to trace
Their shadows, with the magic hand of
Chance;
And when I feel, fair creature of an hour!
That I shall never look upon thee more,
Never have relish in the faery power
Of unreflecting love!—then on the shore
Of the wide world I stand alone, and think,
Till love and fame to nothingness do sink.

That Keats was a poet from the Romantic era was certainly strongly felt in that poem in which the poet attempted to give his feelings about dying young without the opportunity to marry the woman he loved, without family, and without answering some of life's most poignant questions. Yet despite those setbacks in life, his major contributions to poetry were not the words of someone terribly downtrodden, just the opposite—his poems reflected life and hope and exhilaration in the wonder of nature and in a relationship with God or the Divine. For that reason, she understood, he had become one of the world's great poets, and she tried to pass that feeling on to her children as they studied that period of poetry as had been written in the mother country, England.

Leaving thoughts about the Romantic era of poetry for the time being, she came back to her most pressing questions regarding her son, Jesse, the Anointed One. That knowledge—that he was the Anointed One—hadn't come easily. From the moment she received her first visitation from the angel, she knew that her son would be special, but just how special he would become, she had no understanding at first. That knowledge had come to her gradually as she had studied the works of the prophets that were made public, proclaiming the birth of Christ. As she had studied those works, particularly the words of the prophet Isaiah, she had realized that her son, Jesse, was, in fact, the Anointed One himself.

She read and reread the passages from Isaiah in her *Bible* and pondered their meaning and intent. Some of those she had memorized. Most of them spoke of the time leading up to and including the Anointed One's death. It was extremely difficult for her to comprehend how much her son would suffer because of his role in providing for his fellow brothers and sisters a means of salvation, where they could be redeemed from the wages of sin and qualify to return to God's presence and live with him:

> *He is…despised and rejected of men…a man of sorrows…we did esteem him stricken, smitten of God, and afflicted… He was wounded for our transgressions… He was bruised for our iniquities… The chastisement of our peace was upon him…with his stripes we are healed… He was oppressed and afflicted, yet he opened not his mouth… He is brought as a lamb to the slaughter and as a sheep before her shearers is dumb so he opened not his mouth… He was cut out of the land of the living; for the transgressions of my people was he stricken… Made his grave with the wicked and with the rich in his death because he had done no evil, neither was any deceit in his mouth… He hath poured out his soul unto death, and he was numbered with the transgressors; and he bore the sins of many and made intercession for the transgressors…*
> (Isaiah 53:3–12 KJV)

In studying the life of Keats, the poet, and of the Anointed One, Christ, Anne could see a few vague similarities: Christ apparently wasn't married and consequently had no family of his own, was a great teacher, or orator. Keats couldn't be said to be a great teacher or orator but was great with words. Their callings or purpose for life could be argued with some fairness as being divinely appointed, she thought. That's likely where the comparison would end. No one else was even remotely qualified to be the Anointed One. That privilege or calling was only given to one solitary individual, her son, Jesse. In thinking about the weight of that calling, no one could begin to fathom how much weight or pressure that also put upon her as the mother of the Anointed One to see that his calling was fulfilled. She felt that weight press upon her every second of every day ever since she had fully understood the magnitude of what had been given to him. It was not something that could be totally understood by others, including herself.

What to do now, she questioned herself, *to make sure that Jesse went forward, instead of backward? How do I reconcile the family's need to have him with us, against the relevance of his calling? How can I, as his mother, reassure him that the family is totally behind him and willing to give our lives, if necessary, to help him complete his calling? Will it be necessary? Will he have the strength to go forward alone if those close to him betray him by offering not their support or even openly? The time is close*, she concluded, *we will soon know. I must support him whatever he decides to do whenever it happens. I must forget my personal feelings as a mother and support him. I must. I must do so regardless.*

Chapter 42

Darkness and a New Awakening

FOR TWO WEEKS, work at the construction site went forward without a hitch. Jesse and James were in the final days and hours of completing the project. The home was beautiful and would soon be turned over to the buyer. The final inspection and approval of the home by the housing authority was scheduled in only two days' time. They would be ready.

Mary Alice had been vigilant in bringing lunch for the duo, and the two of them were expecting her today at precisely the same time for she was always punctual, even to the minute, without fail and both had come to expect and enjoy the time spent together with her as well as the meal itself for she always managed to add something that was homemade especially for the occasion.

On this day, however, she had failed to show. It was five minutes past the hour in which she always appeared, a bright smile on her face and the promise of a delightful and much-needed break in the rigors of home building. Normally, she appeared with her mother who was used to waiting fifteen to twenty minutes while lunch was eaten in order to bring her home again. Lately, she had been walking again with a two-year-old spaniel the family had purchased to keep her company along the way and ward off attack from others. There had been no further hint of trouble from the girls who had attacked her some time before, and it appeared that that situation had been defused.

When Jesse checked his watch and noted the time, five minutes past the appointed hour when she had promised to appear, he knew immediately that something was wrong. He shouted at James, "*I'm going to find Mary! There's been trouble!*"

He vaulted down from the front steps of the home and ran as quickly as he could along the street on which he knew she would have been coming. He came to the area where she had been attacked by the three girls a few months before, near the post office. She wasn't there.

He turned to the alleyway nearby and started scanning the alley itself. As he moved forward, there was a commotion ahead behind a huge clump of bushes and undergrowth someone had raked together from a backyard just outside a metal double gate. He ran to the point only to find Mary Alice on the ground, unmoving. She was covered with blood from a series of cuts on her upper torso and wasn't breathing. The commotion, he noted, had come from the abrupt disappearance of three girls—probably the same as before—that ran away as he had started up the alleyway. Remains of the lunch she had been bringing to Jesse and James were strewn near her body, and the spaniel was lying nearby, dead from an apparent knife wound.

He sprinted back to the entrance of the alleyway and hailed a man in a brown slouch hat and bib overalls and shouted at him to call 911. "A woman has been beaten in the alley!" he screamed. "She's not conscious and appears dead!"

He ran back to her side and knelt to examine her more carefully. The back of her head and neck were severely bruised and scored from the force of a heavy object. It appeared at first glance to be the cause of death. Moved to act, he took her in his arms and held her tight, willing life back into her body. He didn't know how long he held her; it might have been eight to ten minutes, but finally, he heard sirens screaming along the street heading his way.

Before he knew it, an ambulance crew was at the scene, assessing the situation.

Moments later, Jerrod Houston appeared, screaming, "*Where is Mary! What happened to my daughter!*"

Instantaneous with his appearance, two policemen arrived and, together with the ambulance personnel, separated Jesse from the body of the girl. Blood was everywhere on the victim as well as on Jesse. It was hard to tell who the victim was and who wasn't at first glance.

The ambulance crew—trained paramedics—knelt and quickly searched for a pulse from the slain girl but found none. They began efforts to resuscitate her but finally gave up after two futile attempts.

"*Arrest this man!*" Jerrod Houston screamed. "*He killed my daughter!*" He was hysterical and tried to attack Jesse but was restrained by the two policemen.

The policemen took over and gained control over the situation, separating Houston and Jesse and allowing time and space for the paramedics to put their gear together and begin the notifying of officials that a deceased girl would be transported their way. The larger of the two policemen, a sergeant with the name of *Mason* sewn over his left pocket, his right hand on his service revolver and the left firmly attached to Jesse's left arm, signaled to his blue-clad partner to place handcuffs on Jesse while he held him.

Jesse, reacting to the actions of the two officers, inquired coolly, "Can I tell you what happened here?"

Jerrod Houston interrupted, "*It's very plain what happened. This man attacked my daughter and killed her!*"

"Let him talk!" the senior officer shouted. "He hasn't been charged with anything yet."

"Thank you." Jesse nodded toward the man and began relating what had transpired that led, finally, to him finding Mary Alice's body in the alley. "Three girls ran off as I came close to the spot where she was attacked," he finished. "They were surely the ones who attacked her."

"*That's a lie!*" Houston screamed. "*This man has been stalking my daughter! He is a sex fiend and finally found her alone and killed her. He probably molested her too.*"

"Mary Alice and I are friends, that's all," Jesse replied, continuing, "I found her lying here, and I ran to the street and called for a man to phone 911. If I had killed her, I certainly wouldn't have asked the man to phone the police." He added, "The man probably gave the emergency operator his name. You can verify my story when you locate him." Turning to Houston, he said, "Mr. Houston, I didn't give the man on the street the name of the victim. How is it that you happened to know that your daughter had been attacked?"

Houston struggled to speak. Finally, he blurted, "I was worried when I found out that she was alone. I decided to find her and trailed her to this spot…"

With that, Mason released his grip on Jesse. "Please continue," he said to Jesse, "what else do you know about the situation?"

Jesse paused then looked down on the girl. Kneeling, he took up her arm and said, "She is not dead but is barely conscious. Give her another minute or two, and she will be able to tell you what happened in her own words." He took Mary Alice's two hands and rubbed them carefully with his own. Then wiping his open right hand over her eyes, he watched as they slowly opened and eyelids fluttered. "Mary," he said and she smiled weakly in return, "when you are able, will you tell these men what happened here?"

She coughed weakly twice then whispered, "Yes, I will." And, looking at her father, added, "Jesse, please stay with me."

Chapter 43

The Weird Sisters Talk

AFTER TIME TO recuperate in the hospital, Mary Alice gave the police the names of the three girls who had attacked her, the same girls who had initiated the first attack nearly nine weeks previously. In no time, the girls had been arrested and, being confronted with the news that they had not only been observed but also identified by name, were quick to give the authorities the name of the person who had contacted them, offering payment of $2,000 apiece to assault Mary Alice Houston, "*So that she doesn't get up and walk away, ever,*" as described by the spokes-girl for the group. The name of the person, as given to her, was Marley Davidson, she related, grim faced.

Sheriff Behrenger was involved in the discussion, having been notified by the local police of what had happened, and he had questions of his own after listening to the initial interrogation following arrest. A lawyer from the county attorney's office had been called and had advised the girls to continue to cooperate with the police, hearing the testimony of the girls relating to charges that were being filed, namely, attempted murder.

A quick discussion had followed between the girls and their temporary counsel, who told them a plea agreement might be possible if they were willing to divulge information relating to who it was that had contacted them and promised payment for the attack on the victim. The plea agreement, he had advised them, would probably allow for time in prison with a possibility of early release conditionally based on good conduct. The girls had talked briefly among themselves and then notified counsel that they would tell what they knew about who it was that had contacted them, and that was when Marley Davidson's name had come out.

Advised of the willingness of the girls to cooperate with the officials, Sheriff Behrenger had taken the initiative and asked, "Did the man contact you personally?"

The spokes-girl—the tallest of the three, a plain girl with short, dark hair and hazel, steely eyes that seemed to grow lighter and even more steely as she spoke—had replied, "No, dude. He spoke with us by phone. We received payment according to a plan he set in motion. It was cash, hidden in a secret spot. He was a ghost, you know, man."

"Would you recognize his voice if you heard it again?"

"Yeah, I believe so. It was a deep voice, full and deep, like a bass baritone, man."

"Okay, and he made it clear that she wasn't to survive the attack?"

"That's right, man. It was for keeps."

"Was that all right with you, this business of 'being for *keeps*?'"

"Oh, yeah. He was paying for the job, you know, and we did the job just as he said."

The sheriff thought about telling her that Mary Alice Houston wasn't dead at all but was in the hospital under strict guard but decided to let that be a surprise later.

"We'll have you listen to some recordings of voices later and see if you can identify the voice of the man who contacted you."

"That's cool, man. We'll help you if we can. Do we get to keep the money?"

"That depends."

"Depends on what?"

"Whether you're telling us the truth or not. Also, whether you want to spend blood money for that's what it is. We're going to be checking for prints on the cash. After we're done, you can have it back. How's that?"

"That's cool, man. We're okay with blood money. No one ever asks us where the money comes from. Can I ask you a question, though?"

"Sure, go ahead."

"How is it that we got ID'd? We didn't see any other dudes around, man."

The sheriff glanced at the police and then commented, "You were seen all right, and that person has provided us with a full explanation of what happened. That individual, by request, will remain anonymous until such time as the trial is set in motion and is required to testify."

"So we don't get to know who the dude is?"

"Not unless there's going to be a trial."

"Okay, dude, I guess we can live with that."

"So can the witness." He smiled, and that had ended the preliminary interrogation.

Following the meeting, Sheriff Behrenger went back to his office to consult with his aide, Deputy Roy Collier. "Well, it happened about like we figured," he told the man, "except that the shooter wasn't involved, and the action didn't take place at the construction site." He then told him of the quick appearance of Jerrod Houston after the attack and how that action verified him as the chief suspect in the attack. "He was there to put the blame for the attack on Jesse Christian as quickly as he could. The only problem was, the victim—his daughter—wasn't dead, or was, but was revived later. That's still fuzzy in my mind. How can a person be dead but not dead?" He told him what had happened when the ambulance team arrived and how the girl was pronounced dead after attempts to revive her had failed and how Jesse Christian had knelt at her side and calmly replied that she wasn't dead but barely conscious and had revived her.

"That's quite a trick," the deputy commented.

"It is, and now I'm even more perplexed for that is exactly what that young man must have done when Isaac Christian was shot several weeks ago, that is, brought the man back from the dead and gave him life again. Roy, it appears to me that that young man, Jesse Christian, has power over life and death. Could that be possible?"

166

Collier thought about the question, pivoted in his chair, looked at the perplexed face of the sheriff, and replied, "Not unless he's God."

"Not unless he's God…now there's a thought."

They talked further. The sheriff asked if any progress had been made in tracing the phone number given in the "pest ad" mentioned earlier.

"Some," Collier replied with some reluctance. "I phoned the number, which incidentally is an unclassified number, and got a recording, a short message that had been electronically doctored, I might add, requesting the caller to give information about the 'pest' that was in question as briefly as possible and that the call would be answered soon according to the order in which it had been received."

"Did you give out information about the 'pest'?"

He smiled. "I did. I said, my 'pest' has two legs and growls menacingly when I try and make conversation. I am afraid he might be a new breed of dog and multiply rapidly."

"That's cute. Have you gotten an answer?"

"Not yet but I've done a little checking of unlisted numbers with permission from a friend of mine who works for a federal agency that shall remain nameless, and the phone number can be traced to Jerrod Houston."

"Bingo! That, my friend, makes him the agent for Sydney Ventura as well."

"Exactly!"

The sheriff rubbed his short, grizzled beard then asked, "Is there any way we can trace previous conversations made to that number?"

"Negative, sir."

"That's a shame. Are you sure about that?"

"Not to my knowledge. Also, I'm sure you're aware that we probably can't use the information I just mentioned in a court of law."

"Yeah," he responded grudgingly, "but it gives us a platform to stand on anyway."

"Right."

The sheriff thought for a minute before commenting idly, "I need an eyewitness. Can you provide one for me, one that we can use in court?"

"What about Mary Alice?"

The sheriff scratched his beard again. "She was an eyewitness to the attack on her all right, but will she be willing to testify against her father when she learns that he was responsible for that attack directed at her?"

"I would if it were me."

"Yes, but who knows Jerrod Houston better than his daughter? She knows that he'll stop at nothing to save his company from bankruptcy. She survived one attack. Would she be willing to accept the possibility of another?"

"Maybe, if we can put her father away for a lifetime in prison."

"Yes, but that doesn't preclude the possibility that he can still reach out to others and even the score." He paused. "Is there anybody else who might be willing to stand up to this guy? That's the person we need. Then we can go after his partner, Ted Barrett, and Sydney Ventura… We've got the solution to this thing in our grasp if we play our cards right."

Chapter 44

Sally Comes Forward

THAT AFTERNOON, SALLY Houston knocked at the door of Sheriff Tom Behrenger's office and entered. She had called a few minutes earlier and expressed a desire to meet with the sheriff. He was apprehensive about the meeting, fearing that the woman would present him with an ironclad alibi that her husband wasn't involved in the attempted murder of her daughter. Instead, just the opposite occurred. She sat down and began to explain why she could no longer support her husband in his underhanded tactics to remain in control of the destiny of Houston-Barrett Construction Company.

"Sheriff," she began, "I've put up with a lot of guff from my husband in the twenty-one years we've been married. There has been abuse of all kinds—mental, physical, and sexual—and I've tried to tolerate it and be a loving companion as promised. But I can no longer do that. That abuse has been general, not only on myself but on our two children as well. Now he has gone over the edge. He has attempted to murder his own daughter and place the blame on another. I can no longer stand aside and allow him to do such things. I've got to protect my children, even if it costs my own life, which, I fear, it probably will."

"We can protect you, Mrs. Houston."

"I know. I also know that there's nothing you or your officers could do to prevent him from taking my life if I tell you everything

I know, and he understands where the information has come from. I'm ready to accept that fact. You and a battery of officers won't stop what will ultimately come to pass if I put my husband behind bars."

"Mrs. Houston, I appreciate what you're telling me, and I believe you. Let me also say that you don't have to do this. We're building a good case against your husband and his associate, Tom Barrett. We're going to be able to put a stop to the killing and squash the power by which it's being done."

"Okay," she relented, "but in the meantime, the killing is going to continue, and my children are going to be targeted because they now know the kind of person their father is and what danger that represents for each of them because they've refused to play the game according to his rules."

"You don't have to do this," he repeated, pleading with her.

"Yes, I do, sir." Her face was pallid, taut with tension and with resolve.

"All right." He wiped his face with a checkered handkerchief. "Is it okay if I record your testimony?"

"Of course."

She began talking, telling of all that she knew about her husband's business interests and how those interests had deteriorated badly when the company moved their business holdings into the suburbs. She explained how the company had attempted to subvert the interests of the small construction business in the area owned by Isaac Christian and how her husband had contracted with another to kill Christian after attempts to have the small company merge with them had failed.

She talked of personal insults the man had made to her and to the children because they wouldn't cooperate with him principally in gaining information detrimental to the Christian family. She gave evidence of abuse heaped upon her during the twenty-one years of their marriage and how it had affected her personally as well as on the children, especially Mary Alice. She told how Mary Alice had been groomed to be a party girl, luring others into the bedroom to cement relations between himself, his business, and others.

She alluded to how she and Jerrod had never really had a marriage as such because he had always been working for himself and not for others, how there had never been a vacation for themselves or for the family, or time spent leisurely simply enjoying themselves.

"He is a driven man," she explained, "trained by the military to establish a goal and to plan and implement action to reach that goal despite the odds. He can't accept failure," she explained. "That is not a word in his vocabulary."

"What about his partner, Ted Barrett?" the sheriff asked.

"I don't know much about Ted," she explained. "He keeps to himself, but," she added, "he strikes me as someone with absolutely the same makeup as Jerrod. They are both military men first, last, and foremost. They know only one way to achieve success, 'full speed ahead, and d—— the torpedoes.' I should add, he and Jerrod are first cousins and are thick as thieves, as the saying goes, two of a kind."

The sheriff made some personal notes to himself before continuing. "Do you know anything about Sydney Ventura?" he inquired.

"Oh, you know about Sydney?" she commented.

"Yes, we know about Sydney"—he nodded—"that they were in the military together and that he has been useful to them because of his special talents."

She agreed silently. "Well, how do I begin. Sydney was in the orphanage that was run at one time by Ted's parents. They helped him a great deal, but he turned his back on them and ran away. However, he and Ted and Jerrod have always been close, and as luck would have it, they all three met up in special forces in the military. Jerrod has been careful not to say too much about his 'special talents,' as you mention them. He lives far away, I know, but I couldn't tell you where that is."

"Do you have knowledge of when your husband might have used Sydney recently, say in the attack on Isaac Christian?"

She thought back. "No, I don't, although that sounds like something the three of them put together. Christian was stalked, I know that. I just don't know the particulars."

They talked for a few more minutes before the woman excused herself, saying she needed to get to the hospital to spend time with her daughter. "If you have more questions for me later, sheriff, I would be glad to help."

"Thank you for all you've done, Mrs. Houston," he advised, standing. "You've been a great help. Let me add, would you like to have police custody now? We can make sure that you are protected."

She didn't waver at all. "No, thank you. I will continue as I have before. I need to be a mother to my children. It has been too long that I have allowed them to be ruled by my husband. That has been my great failing in my married life. I'm going to try and make amends to them if I'm given the time. I pray that I will. They are still young and need to have a loving, caring mother."

He opened the door for her. "One other question, ma'am, if you will. Would you be willing to testify in court if that becomes necessary?"

She closed her eyes in thought. "Yes, I will, sheriff. I might as well go the distance full speed ahead. That's the way it's been done in our household…"

Chapter 45

Mary Alice Seeks a New Home

WHEN MARY ALICE was cleared to leave the hospital, she asked that Jesse Christian come and pick her up so that she could go home with him.

Her mother countered with "I'm here, Mary. I can take you home."

"I know, Mom, but I don't want to go home. I want to go with Jesse."

Her mother was hurt at first but then recovered. "You don't want to be around your father, do you?"

She dropped her head and spoke softly, "I'm afraid of him, Mother."

"I know," she imparted, "so am I. I will try and contact Jesse, but, Mary, you'll still be at home with your father."

"No, Mom, I want to stay with Jesse and his family."

"*Mary! You can't do that.*"

"Why not, Mom? They know me and love me. They won't try and kill me…" she added feelingly.

"Mary…" She placed a hand on her daughter's forehead. "I love you too, honey."

"I know, Mom, but honestly, I can't be in the same house with Dad. He'll kill me, I know he will."

"I believe you," she acknowledged. "But, Mary, the Christians have a large family. They can't just throw open their door and say come on in, you're welcome."

"Most would say something like that, Mom, and be sincere, but the Christians aren't like that. They'll find a place for me, you'll see."

"Well, I'll talk to them, okay, and see what they say. I don't know what to tell them, though."

"You don't have to explain anything to them, Mom. They understand my situation. They won't ask for reasons. That's not their way. They look for opportunities to help others."

"Mary, I hope you're right. I'll see what they say, okay? In the meantime, you get your things together and be ready to go by the time I get back.

"Okay, Mom. And, Mom, please don't tell Dad where I am, all right?"

"I won't, honey, but it won't take him long to figure it out if that's where you're going to be."

"I know, but at least I'll be close to Jesse. I love him, Mom, and I know he'll do anything for me."

She couldn't speak, tears ebbing from eyes that couldn't see. "I love you too, honey. Don't you forget that, and, Mary, I'd give my life for you in an instant."

"Thank you, Mom. I hope you don't have to…"

Chapter 46

A Hasty Retreat

JERROD HOUSTON WAS arrested on suspicion of attempted murder. He was allowed to call his lawyer, did so, and appeared before a district judge who was summoned to hear his plea, determine bail, and was summarily set free with instructions not to leave the purlieus of the city.

"I will not," he swore after informing the man that he was entering an initial plea of "no contest."

"There will be a hearing on Friday afternoon at 2:00 p.m.," he was told. "You are to be there with your counsel and be prepared to defend your initial plea. Substantive bail will be set at that time."

* * * * *

As soon as could be arranged, which happened to be that evening, Jerrod got with his partner, Ted Barrett, and summed up what had happened in the last round of action. They were in a vehicle together, in a dark place inside a parking garage on the top floor, nearly void of cars.

"Were you followed?" Barrett questioned.

"Of course. They've been on my tail like hungry hounds ever since this thing started. I lost them, though, when I went through the alleyway on Fourth and Downing. They'll find me, but we've got five minutes or so. I need to talk."

"Hey, this whole thing is topsy-turvy," Barrett began. "We're more exposed than the lead guide in a frontal assault. I'm crazy to meet you. We've got to divide and conquer or else retreat and count our losses, whichever we can. I can't be seen with you. You're poison, you know, and as long as we're together, I'm in this as deeply as you. The only way I can help you is if I can stay out of it. You understand?"

"I do, but don't forget we're partners in this thing. If I go down, you go down with me."

"How can I forget?"

"It was your brilliant idea to go after my daughter. I'm still having a hard time with that. It was lamebrained to strike a deal with those looney girls. They won't stop talking until they've blabbed to the whole world and then some…"

"I know. It was lame, but they contacted me and affirmed Mary Alice's death. Something is screwy. It sounds like what happened when Joseph Christian was shot."

"I know. I swear it happens when the boy, Jesse Christian, is around. Things go screwy in a hurry."

"Maybe he's the one we need to target."

"Maybe so, but this deal with those daffy girls will kill us unless we can pull a rabbit out of a hat and to think that it was my own daughter…"

"Don't act like a saint. You went along with the idea, same as me."

"I did because I had no choice."

"Well, if you had no choice, it was because you screwed up twice before, and I was forced to make a last-ditch effort to get us out of trouble."

"All right, we've both screwed up now. I'll stay in my foxhole, and you stay in yours. Let's see how far we can string this thing out. With help from our lawyers, maybe we can outlast them."

"That's going to be difficult. We're in debt up to our ears, remember? How in the world are we going to pay for our defense? You need to get serious, buddy."

"I'm as serious as I've ever been. If we can't pay for defense, the court will have to appoint us lawyers. We're going to have to use whatever we can get our hands on. Now I've got to go. It's foxhole time, man. Don't let them overrun you. Got it?"

"I've got it. It's h—— or high water."

"Let's go for high water then. Plug your ears and start paddling."

They slapped hands and departed.

Chapter 47

Isaac and Anne Maria at Home

ISAAC WAS THRILLED that the new home was completed along with inspection, and the new owners were preparing to move in. As for himself, he was feeling better and anxious to get back to work. He had another home to build and a second, following that, with the possibility of a third in the foreseeable future. Business was good notwithstanding the unforeseen events which had come his way, roadblocks which he had been forced to deal with. Thinking of those roadblocks, he knew that he wouldn't have been able to deal with them without a good deal of help from Jesse and James as well. The two boys had lifted him up and carried him and his construction business through the heart of the problems that, at first, had seemed insurmountable. He couldn't have been happier at what had happened from within the family to ensure that a home had been built and that a contract had been met on time and with quality work too, work that he could be proud of with no provisos or conditions attached.

He was thinking of ways that he could show his thanks to the boys and the family for all that had been done when Anne came to him and asked for a few minutes of his time.

"Time is one thing I've got a lot of," he replied, smiling.

"Good," she said, sitting beside him on his worn love seat. "We do need to talk."

"About what, dear? You want me to build you a new home?" he offered, a familiar jest between the two of them, something usually brought up when a new home had been finished and sold.

She smiled in turn. "Yes, and please have it finished by next week, will you?"

"I'll certainly do my best, sweetie."

"You are the best, Isaac. Thank you for all you do in helping with the family."

"Well, I haven't been much help lately, I know that. You've been the one who had to do it all, including the office work for the building components, taking care of ordering and of deliveries, and making sure that suppliers were paid. I don't know how you kept up with it all."

"I don't either," she volunteered. "It was touch and go for a while when we weren't sure if we would be able to continue."

"We made it because of you, Anne. No one else could have done what you did."

"Oh, no, Isaac. As a family, we have survived, I'm sure of that. I have to say, though, that Jesse was the one who really kept it all going. Without him, I'm not so sure we could have done what needed to be done. He took James and taught him everything he knew about construction work and did it while shouldering the bulk of the load himself. The boy is so very special. We're going to miss him."

"*Miss him*? It's not time for him to go yet, is it?"

"The time is close. He hasn't said when he's leaving, but I feel that it will be soon. I know that he wants to get away and start his calling and feels ready for the challenges he'll be facing."

"Oh. I'll certainly miss him. He's a lifesaver, I know that."

"I will too," she uttered, teary-eyed. "We all will. There's no one like Jesse…"

"I'm going to go back to work beginning Monday," he informed her, wanting to take her thoughts away from Jesse to help clear her mind.

"Isaac, do you think that's wise? That's only a few days away."

"I know but, yes, I'm ready. I've been loafing around here for too long. I need to start pulling my weight again."

"Oh, you have no idea what it means to be idle. You're always working, doing everything you possibly can, helping others when you don't have anything else to do."

"Thank you for saying so, but you're the one who has kept this family afloat while I've been recuperating. You deserve all the credit."

"Don't forget Jesse. He and the others as well."

"Of course, but this family would have been sorely crippled without you, Anne. You're just too modest to say it."

"You're way too kind, Isaac, but thanks anyway. I do have something I need to talk to you about if this is a good time."

"Certainly. I'm all ears." And he laughed despite himself for he did have rather pendulous ears.

She suddenly became serious. "Jesse has come to me and discussed the possibility of having Mary Alice live with us."

"*Mary Alice?* You're kidding, aren't you?"

"No, he's deadly serious. It was her mother, Sally, who came to me first about the notion and then to Jesse, who in turn talked to me and asked for our support."

"Why, Anne?"

She called upon her reserves of grace in the face of disappointment and challenge and explained in detail what she knew of the Houston household and, specifically, how Jerrod had been treating Mary Alice, along with the threat on her life, which had happened. "She's deathly afraid to go home and be around her father. The man is not rational when it comes to the construction industry. He will do anything to make sure that his company remains in the forefront of the movers and shakers in the field."

"Well, I've experienced some of that for sure. I believe she's right to be afraid to get caught up in his all-or-nothing mania, the end justifies the means."

"Good. I'm glad you see it that way. Do you think that we could work out accommodations for her then?"

He reflected briefly on the home as it was and how it could possibly be altered to invite a guest to come and live with them while keeping privacy as an important factor. "Anne," he said, "it's possible that we could help her, I guess. We've got that small bungalow out back that we sometimes use for visitors or guests. I could do a little work on it and make it suitable for a temporary lodger, I believe, if I could get a little bit of help from the two boys, Jesse and James."

"Would you be willing to do that!" she exulted, her joy bubbling over. "I would certainly like to help the girl. She's in a very bad way with her father, and truly, I like her. And I'm sure that the older boys feel the same way."

"Anne, I don't want to pour any cold water over this whole thing, but thinking about how it might affect her father, I'm afraid that it might put ourselves under the gun as well. Have you considered that?"

Her brow drooped noticeably along with her speech. "Yes, I have, a good deal. I'm also worried, but, dear, we have to help this girl. If we don't, who will? She needs us, and I think our faith will carry us no matter what, don't you?"

"Our faith, yes, and Jesse too. Without him, I wouldn't trust myself. He's the living water that carries us through the storms of life. I hate to think about losing him."

She couldn't have agreed more. Clearing her throat, she said, "All right then, we'll plan on it, and the first order of business will be to make the bungalow suitable for the young lady."

"The young lady...yes."

Chapter 48

A New Home, a New Start

A NUMBER OF significant things happened in the next few days: The bungalow Isaac had referred to in his talk with Anne had been made ready for the expected guest, Mary Alice, and she had moved in with her personal effects. Ted Barrett had been arrested and had gone through the same routine as that experienced by Jerrod Houston, wherein temporary bail had been discussed after an initial plea of "no contest" and his lawyer notified along with a time established to reconvene and determine formal bail and review the plea. He was also warned to stay within the confines of the city and not to leave, to which he had agreed, though terribly unhappy with the situation. The last thing of importance that had happened was that Jerrod Houston had found out that his wife, Sally, had gone to the sheriff, Tom Behrenger, and had testified against him and against his partner, Ted Barrett, as well. For that bit of information, he had become livid beyond comprehension that his wife would go to the authorities and testify against him and against Ted, livid as in a terrible rage.

When he confronted her with the accusation, she replied calmly, "Jerrod, I have pledged to be your companion regardless in this life, but I have never given my word that I would support you if you sought the lives of my children. And that is what has happened. I will not, I cannot, support you when you plan or attempt to murder my children. That is not part of the deal! You may do what you want with me with or without the consent of the law, I suppose, and I will suffer the consequences. But I will not stand idly by and watch my children be murdered!"

"It was not my idea…" he began weakly to defend himself.

"Maybe not," she countered, "but you certainly didn't do anything to try and stop it."

"You'll be sorry, Sally," he promised, his rage mounting.

"I'm sure you're right, and I'm also sure that I'll be the next target, instead of the others. But I'm ready to pay that price. All I ask is that you leave the children alone."

"You can't ask for anything from me, Sally. You've already taken a stand against me. Now you've got to suffer the consequences. I'm not the kind of man who forgets things like this."

"Oh, I know that all right. I knew that when I went to Sheriff Behrenger. I'd do the same thing again if I had to, to save the lives of my children."

"You may have lost them anyway!" he swore and turned and left.

One good thing had happened, however, to offset those things which had been monumentally bad for the Houston-Barrett Construction Company: Mary Alice had been accepted into the family of Isaac and Anne Christian and had been treated with queenly acceptance for which she was ever so grateful. She worried about the welfare of her mother and of Bailey, the younger brother, but at least now she could take a deep breath and relax, knowing that she was in the company of good people who loved her and would look out for her. That assurance meant the world to her at present.

That night, the family had gotten together and talked, each of the children reciting some small bit of information about themselves that she hadn't heard before. That simple revealing of oneself had brought her closer to each of the children, including the older ones. It had started innocently enough and then had blossomed into something that filled her with a spirit she had never felt before, a feeling of love and belonging she had never encountered, a feeling of family, of worth, and of happiness through the simple act of opening one's heart to others.

Jeri, for instance, had talked about the time that Jesse had reassured her of his love through the act of holding hands and how that act had bonded the two of them together in a way that couldn't be explained by words. Her younger brother, Joseph, had spoken of an incident more recent when word had come to him about the shooting of Isaac and how his father was close to death. With tears in his eyes, he told of how a voice had come into his mind, stating that his father would live, would be with him again soon. James had talked about how he had formed ill feelings about her, Mary Alice, saying he was sorry for all that he had said or done that might have reflected that feeling and how he had changed his feeling to one of love and admiration for her and that he was sorry. He was so sincere that it brought tears to Mary Alice as she heard his simple confession.

John had surprised her by saying that he loved her because she was so pretty and nice, and he wanted to find someone like her as he grew older to be with *for a long time*. He told how he had worked extra hard when asked to do so in the bungalow to make it a swell place for Mary Alice because he wanted her to be happy.

When it became Jesse's turn, she listened intently, wondering what he would say.

His face flushed after he began what sounded almost like a prayer being uttered. "I have asked for faith and strength to be able to help others. Mary Alice has been an answer to prayer. She has needed my help, and I'm glad that I've been able to give that help. It has been such a good thing for me, helping me draw closer to my Heavenly Father. I want to continue to help her if that is possible. I hope that we can be together *for a long time*, as John said," and smiled at her.

When it came time for her particular "self-portrait," as the experience had been presented, she found that she didn't have any difficulty opening her heart to the others. The hard part was controlling her emotions to be able to talk and be heard.

She started, "I feel so much love with this family. It's something I've never experienced before. It's wonderful and makes me want to fill my heart with that same emotion forever. I want to be close to each of you. As a child, I was raised to be good at creating illusions, false impressions that would lead others to do or commit to certain things that would benefit me or my father because he was always directing me toward that end. So my life was a lie really, a pretense, a weak imitation of the truth. With each of you and especially Jesse because he was the first who introduced me to genuine love for others, I want to say thank you. Each of you have touched me in ways I can't begin to explain for good, for honesty, and for love…" And she broke down and couldn't speak.

The others crowded around her and smiled and wept in turn.

"This is family…" she uttered.

Finally, Isaac and Anne each expressed how thankful they were to be able to reach out to Mary and help her when help was needed. They also expressed a wish to be able to help Sally and Bailey if the time were right and that her father wouldn't be offended.

Glowing with admiration and the sweet spirit of love and companionship, the family concluded the evening with the simple time-worn game of "pin the tail on the donkey." They were each blindfolded and spun around so that they couldn't begin to imagine where they were in the room or where the donkey was situated on an easel and moved around with each change of person. The results were hilarious, and the family laughed and cried with abandon as each blundered here and there to find the donkey and get the tail on that animal in the right place.

Lastly, Anne brought out a treat of cookies and ice cream. That was a fitting way to end the evening.

When time came for good nights to be said, everyone was surprised when Jesse commented, "I'm going to be gone for a couple of days. I need to be alone, to decide when I'll be leaving," and his gaze swept around the room where a silence had fallen upon all who listened with what was suddenly hearts so heavy they seemed to have fallen on the floor.

Chapter 49

A World Blown Apart

MARY ALICE HAD experienced a great many highs and lows in her short life similar to the agony and ecstasy of most teenagers. What she had experienced so far, however, was nothing to what was on the horizon. When she went to bed that night following the "family night" activities, she had felt wonderfully accepted by the Christian family and, along with that, a feeling of wellness and acceptance without parallel, something she had never felt before and didn't dream possible. Her happiness had been abruptly tempered, however, by the announcement that Jesse would be leaving to spend time with his "father" and that the meeting between the two individuals would determine when the son, Jesse, would be leaving his Christian family for good. That was a crushing blow to her, something she hadn't thought about before, something she didn't want to consider at all.

She moped through the following day, saddened further by the communication passed along by Anne that Jesse had already left by the time she had gotten up and that he had left no special message or instructions for her, no hint of love or of love lost, or anything else but had vanished from her life without a trace of emotion whatsoever, temporarily anyway.

So that she was hardly prepared for the next bit of news that she received, news that woke her from a light, troublesome sleep the next morning at 4:22 a.m., when Sheriff Tom Behrenger appeared at the door of her bungalow with Anne Maria Christian and excused himself as the bearer of bad news: "*I'm sorry to have to inform you, Mary Alice, that an explosion destroyed your parents' home earlier tonight and both of your parents are dead.*"

"*What!*"

"Yes, it is true. Your father was apparently working in the garage-workshop area late last night and ignited some highly flammable material, causing an explosion that rocked the home and caused a fire to sweep through the entire house. Your father was virtually incinerated, and your mother was able to get out but died later due to asphyxiation in the hospital. Your brother, Bailey, wasn't at home and is all right. He is currently with a friend."

Mary Alice couldn't talk. She wasn't even able to think properly for a while until she finally struggled to the main house in Anne's arms to be comforted until such time as she could gather herself and check on Bailey, phoning to make sure the boy was all right.

When the crying finally subsided, she asked, "Is Jesse home yet?"

"No," Anne replied, trying desperately to hide her disappointment.

"I need him," she uttered and began crying again.

"He should be home sometime today," she offered, hoping it was true.

The sheriff came again later in the afternoon, along with his deputy, Roy Collier, and spent time with her and with Anne and Isaac, who had stayed close to Mary Alice and Bailey as well, who was now with his sister. The two of them had been extremely solicitous in helping both children deal with the deaths of their parents.

When Mary Alice asked again how the explosion and fire was ignited, the sheriff took a deep breath and speculated, "We're not sure yet, but it appears that your father was making some kind of explosive device," he informed her. "We've found highly volatile traces of what he must have been working with dynamite, gunpowder, and nitroglycerin. We don't know what caused the explosion. We speculate that he may have attempted to light a cigarette. It is known that your father was a serious smoker. That is correct, isn't it?"

She nodded without answering.

"He may have begun to light a cigarette, forgetting how explosive the materials were that he was using in his device or thinking that he was a safe distance away."

She nodded again.

Bailey, however, asked, "Why would he be building a bomb, sir?" The boy was struggling to understand the dynamics of the situation.

"We're not sure, son. There are elements of this that have escaped us so far. We'll attempt to put it all into perspective as soon as possible and let you know. Right now, we simply don't have all the answers."

"Where is my mother?" Mary Alice asked.

"Her body is in the morgue now. She was at the hospital while they attempted to resuscitate her, but since that failed, they transferred her body to the morgue."

She dropped her head and wept silently. "I wish Jesse had been here," she intoned quietly.

"We've tried to contact him," Anne imparted, "but so far, we haven't been able to reach him."

"He should be home soon," Isaac added.

"How long will they keep her body in the morgue?" Mary Alice asked.

"They will keep it frozen—the body—and then wait for the family—for you, Mary—to inform them about which undertaker or funeral home you would like to deal with."

She nodded.

"I will help you, Mary," Anne contributed. "There are things that will need to be done, such as dressing her if there is to be a funeral."

"Thank you," she whispered and wiped her eyes and nose. After a quiet moment of reflection, she asked, "Was she badly burned?"

He brightened a bit. "No, she wasn't. She must have gotten out of the house in good time after the initial explosion. Apparently, however, after she was clear of the house, she went back into the house or garage area, possibly looking for her husband or Bailey. We don't think she went directly into the fire but must have gotten close enough that smoke inhalation became a serious problem. That is what we think anyway."

"Did she know that you weren't in the house, Bailey?" she asked, looking at Bailey.

"I-I think so. I left them a note anyway."

"Where did you put the note?"

He thought back then stuttered, "I'm not sure... I may have forgotten to put it where it could be found."

"That may be the answer to why she went back to the house. She was looking for Bailey," the deputy concluded.

"I-I guess so," Bailey concurred hesitantly.

Jesse didn't come back that night. Isaac and Anne Maria brought a cot to the bungalow so that Bailey and Mary Alice could be together during the interval before morning. They were doing all they could to help the two siblings feel at home and be comforted. Mary Alice, however, appeared to be beyond consolation of any kind. She was extremely distraught, not necessarily for her father but for her mother, Sally, and, of course, how the deaths of the two parents would affect both her and Bailey but primarily Bailey.

When morning finally broke with the appearance of a sliver of light in the eastern horizon, she hadn't slept. She had cried herself out, though, and was ready for the worst, whatever that represented, when a teenage girl suddenly finds herself without home or parents, a waif with no job, and few friends, except those who had come close to her recently and shown her love and support. She knew, however—or thought she knew—that she wouldn't be able to stay with the Christian family for an extended period of time, especially not with Bailey at her side who also needed a home and parental support and love, which she would have to provide until such time as he was able to provide for himself, maybe five to ten more years. It wasn't simply her parents' home that had blown up; it was her own as well and Bailey's.

They had finished a quiet breakfast and washed and put the dishes away when Jesse walked into the home. He went to Mary Alice immediately after entering and held her in his arms.

She started to explain but he interrupted with "I know, Mary. I'm so sorry."

"*You know?*"

"Yes, I know." He was tired. Had walked most of the night. "When you feel that you're ready, take me to your mother."

"Jessie," she wailed, "if you had been here…"

"It's going to be all right, Mary," he entreated imploringly.

* * * * *

Isaac and Anne took Jesse and Mary Alice and Bailey to the funeral home when it was discovered that her body had just been transferred from the morgue to the funeral home so that preparations for burial or cremation could be made. When they got to the funeral home, they walked in together and introduced themselves, Mary Alice and Bailey, as children of the deceased. Soon after the introductions were concluded, Jesse asked where the body was being kept.

When he was directed to a room adjacent to the entryway, he asked, "As a close friend of the family, may I see the body for a few minutes alone?"

Startled by the question, the funeral home director looked at Mary Alice for confirmation, seeking consent for the unusual request. She was as surprised as he was but nodded her consent. Accordingly, Jesse walked into the room and quietly closed the door.

"What is he going to do?" the funeral director asked.

"I don't know," Mary replied, bewildered as the others.

"He is a man of God, a holy man," Anne explained. "He likely wants to pray over her."

That seemed to satisfy the man, but after a few minutes of forced silence, he asked, "Is he still praying?"

Isaac and Anne both nodded together.

"Be patient," Isaac inserted hopefully. "He's surely finishing the prayer."

They waited another five minutes.

Finally, the funeral director said, "I'm going in there."

Just as he began to move, the door opened, and Jesse and Sally walked out of the room together, arm in arm. She was smiling, her face bright with excitement and life, and rushed forward to gather her two children about her like an angel of mercy, kissing each and smothering them with affection as they melted into her arms, rapt in joy.

Chapter 50

Of Healing and Recovery

THE NEXT TWO weeks were a blur in Mary Alice's mind. The Christian family had spent that time enlarging the bungalow so that Sally and Bailey could stay with Mary Alice, at least until further arrangements could be made.

"You're welcome to stay as long as you like," they had been told. "The place is yours, and you are our guests."

One of the first orders of business had been the requiem for Jerrod, unannounced and largely unknown, except to a few close friends. Isaac and Jesse had spent a few hours the day before the official ceremony was to be held, making a suitable coffin out of cedar, resplendent with variegated coloring—tan to dark brown—beautifully polished and oozing with a powerful scent that could only be described as unique to that type of wood when sanded and highly polished, coated lightly with resin.

There was no one there to preside, but Isaac addressed the small group, as petitioned by Sally, and asked that remembrances of Jerrod be shared. He began with a short vignette of the man, saying that he was a no-nonsense individual who had put his heart and soul into his work, the same as he had done while serving in the military for his country. "He was a lover of hard work and industry, and when duty called and his country needed his help, he was quick to respond. We need more men like that in today's army."

A few others expressed similar thoughts, and when the last was said, a song and prayer concluded the occasion.

Two days after the hasty service, the sheriff contacted Sally and asked if she could meet with him and his deputy to wrap up some of the details that had become apparent since the death of Jerrod Houston.

She agreed and asked if Mary Alice and Jesse could come as well since Mary had made the request after consulting with Jesse and was told that it would be all right. Sally and Mary Alice had both thought that Jesse should be allowed to be there since he was involved so closely.

As the proposed meeting got underway in a private room at the county headquarters inside the sheriff's office, the sheriff and his chief deputy, Roy Collier, greeted the others. "Thanks for coming. This shouldn't take too long. We simply want to inform you folks of information that has come to light since your husband's death, Mrs. Houston. We do this because we know that you've been under some duress over what has happened since our earlier discussion and because your husband had threatened you prior to his death, as you explained, the day of his passing."

Sally had warned Mary Alice earlier that some unflattering things would be said about her father and that she should prepare herself emotionally. She had agreed, saying, "Mother, I won't be surprised. I lived with him almost as long as you did. Remember?"

"Thank you. Yes, it has been a difficult time, wondering what plans he had made and how those plans were to be put into operation, whether those plans stopped with his death or not."

"Exactly. Well, let me brief each of you on what we've learned since that time, meaning his untimely death."

"I'm not so sure it was untimely," she offered, "but go ahead."

The sheriff smiled in acknowledgment, recognizing that the man's death had really been a godsend to each of them, regardless of relationship to Jerrod Houston. "I'm going to defer to my deputy, Roy Collier, here to bring you up-to-date in the elements of this case which affect each of you as well as ourselves." He turned to Collier and pointed with an open hand.

Collier began, "We were fortunate to be able to recognize the presence of Sydney Ventura at your husband's requiem, Mrs. Houston. He was in disguise, but we saw through the disguise and confronted him. He is currently in custody and facing several charges of murder for hire along with other lesser charges, such as tax evasion. He is cooperating so far, and his further cooperation may be enough to keep him alive anyway, though a lengthy prison term is probable. On the plus side, he was an excellent soldier, and his record as such speaks highly for him.

"Ventura has made no statement yet, except to say that he and Barrett and Houston were friends. What evidence we have against him is mostly circumstantial, but we've been informed that the FBI is thrilled that we've got him in custody. They have been searching for him for some time, it turns out, and so we've turned over our files to them. Apparently, he had a dual purpose in coming to the services, wanting to pay his respects to Houston at his passing and wanting to be paid for the botched attempt on Isaac's life. He had to be surprised—and that's putting it mildly—to find out that his friend, Houston, was the person who arranged the attack on Isaac Christian and had refused payment following the attack.

"We also have Tom Barrett in custody. We were able to intercept a phone call from Barrett to Ventura, informing the latter of the death of Houston and, in doing so, build a case for the three individuals who have been at the forefront of a syndicate for crime and corruption, essentially murder for hire, as indicated. That was how we were able to plan for his arrest at the informal rites for Houston. Barrett, we add, also has a sterling military record, which is in his favor, similar to Jerrod Houston, as has been mentioned already. We used phone conversations and sophisticated speech-patterning devices to tie Barrett to the man who introduced himself as Marley Davidson—an alias—in the attempted murder of Mary Alice here."

"So it was Barrett and not my father who planned my death?"

"Yes, although your father certainly knew what was going on and likely agreed with the action." The man paused and looked at the others, scanning their faces, and then at Sheriff Behrenger. "Anything else, Tom?"

The sheriff focused on Sally before adding, "We teach them how to kill in the military, how to be professional killers. There are quite a few who can't do that sort of thing. They eliminate themselves in a hurry and end up working at desks or as clerks or other odd jobs. Some learn better than others. Some die mentally, even spiritually, before they can learn how to cope with the power given to them to destroy a person's life. Some can't stop killing when given a release from the military. Maybe they've been trained too well. It's a terrible thing what men do to each other when they become trained assassins. In order to succeed, to become horribly efficient, a person has to act and not think to effectively abolish all thoughts of humanity to man, to become animalistic and adopt the maxim, 'kill or be killed' or 'survival of the fittest.' It's all the same. When they say 'war is hell,' it is really an understatement, in my mind anyway. I'm sorry if that's too graphic."

"We're all victims in a way," Sally interposed, "the trained killers, the ones who die, and those who are part of the family of each who are trained in that manner."

The sheriff nodded and continued, "It does appear, from all that we've been able to learn from the effects of the fire along with information received about threats made prior to the fire, that Jerrod Houston was planning another violent act, probably your death, Sally, and perhaps even the deaths of yourself and your two children. He was desperate and desperate men do desperate things, things that aren't rational to others. I believe he was in that irrational state when he was preparing the bomb that would destroy his family and home."

There was a protracted silence that followed the sheriff's statement before a voice rose from the ashes of despair, as it were from the ashes.

The voice was Collier's, and he asked, staring directly at Jesse, "How is it that you've been able to bring dead men and dead women back to life? That is something I can't understand for the life of me. I'm not sure if that's a pun or hyperbole or just simply a paradox, but please answer if you will."

Each of them trained their eyes on Jesse, wondering how he would answer. Suspense hung in the air like the tick of a time bomb before it exploded.

Jesse thought of the question, smiled, and replied, "Jerrod Houston was the agent for Sydney Ventura, and that worked well for those men until now. I have been summoned to act as agent for God, who has all power even over death. That works even better when needed."

That signaled the end of the meeting.

Chapter 51

A New Beginning

JESSE AND MARY Alice were together outside the county building. The others were mingling with each other a short distance away. The sheriff had followed them outside and was still fielding a few questions that hadn't been answered yet.

Mary Alice was heartbroken. A life had been saved but another was dead and, worse, for her, a life was about to be lost. Not hers but Jesse's since he would be leaving her.

"You're leaving, aren't you?" she said, crying inside.

"Yes."

"Will it be soon then?"

"As soon as I can gather my things."

"Where will you go?"

He looked away. "I'm not sure, Mary, wherever the Spirit calls me."

She closed her eyes and attempted to think of what lay ahead for him and for her. "Will you have a home anywhere? How will I be able to contact you?"

He shook his head. "No home, Mary. I will be moving from one place to another…"

"Will you have some followers with you?" she asked hopefully.

"Yes, I think so. There will be those who will follow me as soon as I can become more established, teaching God's Word. They will believe in me and what it is I have to give to others."

She held back the tears, breathlessly hoping for his will to include her, asking, "Can I be one of your followers, *Lord?*"

He picked up on the term "*Lord*" and what it meant. "You call me *Lord?* Do you know the significance of that term?"

"Not fully, but of you, I believe it fits. You are my Lord, Lord of all, the greatest, Lord of Lords."

He reached out and held her shoulders, feeling her resolve. "To go or to stay is a question you must ask yourself, Mary, and your mother. I can't answer it for you, but you must understand that, according to the prophets, my life will be filled with deep sorrow, such as no man or woman has ever experienced before. There will be brief moments of joy too, of course, but the sorrow will last until it is finally overcome by joy in the end, long after earth life is concluded. It will not be easy to be close—a follower—while the sorrow prevails. There will be those who will seek to kill me, even from within. They might want to kill you as well if you follow me. I can't protect you all the time and remain on my father's errand. In the end, what I do, I must do myself with no help to the end. It must be that way."

She let the tears out. She could hold them no longer. "I am willing to die for you, *Lord.* Is that enough?"

He held her close and whispered, "Thank you, Mary. That is enough and more. However, only the Father can decide who is to die and who is not as part of his great plan for mankind. I have agreed to give my life for you and for the others, for everyone. It will not be easy, but I will bear the burden alone. If I fail, God's plan to bring his children back home will also fail unless another comes forward and takes my place. I'm not even sure that's possible. No more will be asked of you than to be a follower." He drew a breath and released her, smiling. "Are you sure you want to do this?"

"Yes, Lord. I will go and I will be a follower to the end. Mother will not say no, not when I explain how I feel."

"We will go together then, and we will support each other in the difficulties ahead. I will be a strength for you, and you can give me comfort when it is needed."

She blinked back the tears. "You have hinted about your father. You must remember that I'm what you would call a neophyte as far as religion is concerned, but you have promised that you would tell me of your father and, hopefully, of your relationship with him, what that means to you now as you begin to go forward with your calling or whatever it is that you must do."

"Yes, I remember, and I did promise you, Mary. First let me say that you and I have the same father…"

"What? How is that possible?"

"That is what I must explain to you. This is going to take some time, I'm afraid."

"I have the time, Jesse. In fact, I have the rest of my life. Will that be enough?"

He smiled again. "That should work all right, but we must start right away without losing any time."

"Good. I'm anxious for the first lesson."

And so they sought out a place of solitude where they wouldn't be interrupted, and he began, "In the beginning…"

Epilogue

WHEN CHRIST, THE Anointed One, was on the cross following the betrayal by Judas—one of his followers—the Master spurned the use of force to defend him. The sword of Peter, his chief apostle, had been sheathed, according to an order given by the Savior. He would not have his disciples forfeit their lives for him at that time until the *Word*, his gospel, had been preached to the known world. Following that great missionary effort, their time would come when persecution against his teachings would reach such an avalanche of force that no one would live who avowed themselves as Christians, followers of Christ. To those zealots, Christ was the heretical one, the one who claimed to be the Son of God, the one who healed others who raised the dead, and did those things by the power of the devil.

While a multitude of onlookers gathered at Calvary to watch the spectacle of Christ's death, he was nailed to a wooden cross. He had been scourged, or beaten, with a whip prior to that. He had been abused in different ways besides, spit upon, forced to wear a crown of thorns, and given vinegar instead of water to drink.

Among the crowd at his feet were the two principal women who had been with him in life, Mary, his mother, along with Mary Magdalene, who had given support through his trials and who hadn't refrained from a willingness to give all whatever was necessary to support him to the very end.

At the last, while on the cross, the Lord called for help from his Father. With all the strength he had left, he called for help. He could have called for a host of angels—legions—to come and help would have been given. In the end, however, his calling, his mission to save you and me from sin, would have been aborted. His life would have been in vain. He could not do that. He called to his father for help so that he could endure the agony to the end, that his atonement for mankind would be acceptable.

To have received an interposition of help at that time would have meant that Christ's life was in vain, his suffering without purpose. Christ, the Son, had to pay the price for you and for each of us in turn. He had to go through the agony of the cross and all that it represented by himself without intervention from his Father (John 3:16–17 KJV, see also I Corinthians 15:22 KJV).

Even so, he continued to cry out, beseeching the Father for aid until, at last, his heart burst. That mighty heart which carried with it the joys and sorrows of all mankind burst, and the Lord slumped and died, his earthly mission fulfilled successfully.

Peter's sword was still in its sheath. Peter, the man, was busy hiding not wishing to be seen with Christ and stamped a Christian. Later, he gained courage and died in the same manner as Christ, on the cross, according to tradition. But at that time, he was not with Mary and the other Mary, who kept a lonely vigil at the feet of Christ together with John the Beloved, who was given charge by Jesus to look after his mother. At Christ's death, the earth cried out, mountains came down, seas over swept their boundaries, valleys became hills and mountains, and rocks became pebbles of sand, and vice versa. All was in tumult. The Lord of heaven and earth had died, and earth couldn't hide its disappointment. The angels were reverently quiet. There was no singing of anthems of praise, *but God had prevailed! In three days, Christ would live again, and at that moment, the hosts of heaven would shout for joy!*

Amidst the drama surrounding Christ's death and subsequent resurrection, the disciple who betrayed Christ, Judas Iscariot, climbed a tree and hung himself. He didn't wait for any contrived earthly tribunal to pronounce sentence upon him for his act of perfidy. He found himself guilty. The saying is true, "Man, by himself is priced for thirty pieces Judas sold himself, not Christ."

There are some comparisons that can be drawn from the life of Roland, his death, and the life and death of Christ, although it is admittedly far-fetched. Roland is considered a mythical figure; some argue that Christ, though a great teacher, was not the Son of God. Roland couldn't have saved his life, whereas Christ had the power to live on, not to submit to death. He also had power over death through the resurrection as directed by his Father. Both Roland and Christ were great in their respective situations: Roland, representing the person who is an advocate for Christ and his teachings, and Christ, the author of those teachings. Let it rest at that until Judgment Day when, according to Christian theology, each of us will be summoned to the Bar of God to be judged of our works, whether they be good or whether they be evil.

There will be the followers of Christ, and there will be those who profess followship but lag behind; and lastly there will be those who have fought against the Anointed One, the King, the Redeemer of Israel.

Christians contend that all will live again because of Christ's atoning sacrifice. They happily imagine a mansion awaiting all who are saved by God and his grace. The joy of heaven will welcome each who has faith to accept God and his laws and commandments into their lives, choosing to abide those published teachings. Until then, may God be with you as his follower, and, if not, may your notion of God achieve for you all that you have imagined is good and of benefit to mankind in the hereafter. It's bound to please you in that event.

Of note, James, Christ's brother, was firm in his testimony of Christ. Though not a part of recorded history, it has been published that he died as Stephen did, stoned to death. It may well be that his other brethren died in much the same manner, as followers of Christ, to the end.

As for Mary Magdalene, not much is known of her life following the events of the death and resurrection of Christ along with his ascension. It has been said that she followed Peter and the other disciples to France later, where they hid for a time in a cave. It is believed that she remained a faithful witness for Christ throughout those lonely years as she followed the disciples who proclaimed the

truths of the gospel established by Christ no matter the consequences
There is no record of her having married.

I have taken license to portray her as a seductress, a loose
woman, in this paper. That notion is without foundation. No one
really knows what it was that caused seven demons to take possession
of her body, no one but God really. She was a good woman, I believe
that sincerely. Christ made that goodness shine.

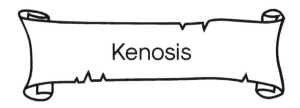

Kenosis

If you begin with God the Heavenly One
And send him to earth,
Subjecting him to temptation and pain,
And oppress him until he hath no place
To lie his head,
And he becomes a man of grief and sorrows,
Rejected by his own, despised and spit upon,
And take away his vesture and scourge him,
So that he loses his comeliness,
Marred and disfigured,
And nail him upon a cross,
Then you have the death of God the Son,
Who made an offering for sin
For you and me.

The Carpenter

Is not this the carpenter the son of Mary?
He who laboreth with his hands to frame monuments to man.
The mortise and tenon he knoweth well, as pith and marrow.
Spikes and timbers he worketh artfully as sinew and bone.
The fulcrum he understandeth, the arch, the carpenter's rule.
The hammer and handsaw are not strangers to his work, nor the
        brace and bit.
The miter box, the plumb bob, the bellows and forge all fit
His calloused hands.
Mortar and pestle he useth often as cortex and skin.
Beams he carefully shapeth with chisel and awl into trusses
That support the mass.
His practiced eye judgeth a wall as truly as any with blueprints
As a guide.
Shoulders broad and toned easeth rafters into place.
The footing, the headboard, the capstone, the temple, all,
He fitteth with a craftsman's lore.
What think ye of this weathered carpenter, this Nazarene
Who worketh with his hands?

About the Author

THE AUTHOR AND his wife, Sylvia, reside in a small northeastern community called Holbrook, named after a former railroad employee, probably an agent. They graduated from Holbrook High School in 1960, hand in hand, and married in 1964. At graduation, he was distinguished as All-Around Boy, and she was likewise distinguished as All-Around Girl.

Both Richard and Sylvia graduated from Arizona State University in Tempe, Arizona, where they received their teaching credentials. The couple moved back to Holbrook in 1984 when invited by then Superintendent of Schools Frank L. Turley to become part of the Holbrook School District teaching staff. Sylvia retired in 2008, and Richard followed shortly after in 2009.

They have seven children, four boys and three girls. Richard spends free time writing, both prose and poetry; and Sylvia keeps track of the sons and daughters and their respective families scattered in Colorado, Utah, and Arizona.